The State to Come

Will Hutton is the editor of the *Observer*. A former stockbroker, he spent ten years with the BBC and from 1983 to 1988 was economics correspondent for BBC 2's 'Newsnight'. He was economics editor of the *Guardian* from 1990 and became assistant editor in 1995. He was nominated Political Journalist of the Year by Granada Television's 'What the Papers Say' for his coverage of the 1992 ERM crisis. His book on Keynesian economics, *The Revolution That Never Was*, was published in 1986, and the bestselling *The State We're In* in 1995.

He is member of the governing council of the Policy Studies Institute, the Institute for Political Economy and is a governor of the London School of Economics. He is a visiting professor at Manchester Business School, a visiting fellow at Nuffield College, Oxford, and is on the editorial board of *New Economy*. In 1995 he became Chair of the Employment Policy Institute. Will Hutton is married with three children.

BY WILL HUTTON

The Revolution That Never Was
'Good Housekeeping: How to Manage Credit and Debt' (IPPR)
The State We're In
The State to Come

Will Hutton

THE STATE TO COME

Published by Vintage 1997

2 4 6 8 10 9 7 5 3 1

First published in Great Britain by
Vintage, 1997

Vintage
Random House, 20 Vauxhall Bridge Road, London SW1V 2SA

Random House Australia (Pty) Limited
20 Alfred Street, Milsons Point, Sydney,
New South Wales 2061, Australia

Random House New Zealand Limited
18 Poland Road, Glenfield,
Auckland 10, New Zealand

Random House South Africa (Pty) Limited
Endulini, 5A Jubilee Road, Parktown 2193, South Africa

Random House UK Limited Reg. No. 954009

A CIP catalogue record for this book
is available from the British Library

ISBN 0099778815

Papers used by Random House UK Ltd are natural, recyclable products made from wood grown in sustainable forests. The manufacturing processes conform to the environmental regulations of the country of origin

Set in 10½/12 Sabon by SX Composing DTP, Rayleigh, Essex
Printed and bound in Great Britain by
Mackays of Chatham PLC, Chatham, Kent

A VINTAGE ORIGINAL

Contents

For Jane and the family

PREFACE

NOBODY COULD HAVE been more surprised than me at the success of *The State We're In*, but, as one leading politician had warned me soon after publication, I found that it became a book against which people carefully positioned themselves. You could not only be broadly for or against its basic analysis and arguments, but even those who were pro would position themselves judiciously as more level-headed, market friendly and centrist than its determinedly loyal Keynesian author (unreconstructed to my critics) – or more radical.

So it has proved, and the politician in question became one of the leading position-takers. I have no complaints: it's been stimulating and great fun. But in the approach to and immediate aftermath of what promises to be a key general election I have become increasingly concerned that all this positioning has led to a bastardisation of the book's arguments – and a weakening of the arguments for stakeholding. Indeed much of the criticism seems in inverse proportion to the thoroughness with which *The State We're In* has been read, preferring instead to go by the reviews and general mood music, which themselves are part of the positioning game. In any case, nearly three years have passed since I completed it, and the arguments need to be revisited and refreshed.

So this short book is the result of those concerns. It casts a cool and sceptical eye over the Conservative 'achievement', and examines quite why contemporary British capitalism has the character it has. Chapter 3 examines how it could be reformed, organising economic, social and political initiatives as a linked whole, in terms non-specialists, I hope, can easily understand. Some of the emerging figures on inequality are breathtaking; we do live in a fundamentally unfair society and a run-down democracy. There must be change. Some of my fellow advocates of stakeholding do not go as far either in their analysis or in their remedies, preferring instead to talk generally about changing the culture. But if we can't develop a robust policy programme, then we're no help to anybody. This is the best effort I have made so far at defining how a stakeholder economy and society might be built but it is still very much work in progress.

This emphatically does not mean constructing the current German economy in Britain, returning to 1970s corporatism or wishing – as allegedly an inveterate 'declinist' – for a better yesterday. Nor does it mean cherry-picking bits of best practice from around the globe and importing them into Britain with no regard for how they worked abroad. It accepts that the economy and society are ineluctably built around the market, but tries to shape the institutions, incentives and culture of the market system by looking for the appropriate triggers. The implication, as I said in *The State We're In*, is that we start from where we are and do things that are congruent with our very specific Britishness. It also means, and I have grown more convinced of this over the last three years, that to enlarge its options Britain must be a full-hearted player in the European Union, which even includes membership of the single currency.

I hope the book will be seen as an optimistic, can-do, forward-looking study – for that is very much how I feel. There is every chance now of a change of government, and with it the once-in-a-generation opening that occurs in British politics before the traditional Conservative blanket settles over us again. We can build a better country, which would make everything – from travelling to work to educating our kids – much less harrowing than it is at present. If the book contributes just a little to hardening the resolve of voters and politicians alike, and pushing on the debate about policy, it will have done its job.

The State to Come was written over five weeks, completed

on 9 March. I am acutely aware of how it could have been improved with more time, but neither the election timetable nor my responsibilities at the *Observer* allowed it. As a result I have needed very quick reactions from friends who have agreed to read it in draft, and I have been lucky that they have been so prompt. Martin Jacques and David Held both offered extensive criticism and valuable suggestions; David Miliband faxed me a typically well-constructed critique at my hotel during a so-called holiday in the middle of writing, as did David Held. Neil Belton had some important reactions, and I appreciated my personal telephone seminars on reflexivity with Anthony Giddens and Geoff Mulgan. John Gray, both in conversation and in the draft of his forthcoming book, helped to crystallise my ideas – especially on globalisation; and Colin Mayer is a boundless source of articles and contacts. David Halpern and Stuart White produced two very useful papers with important suggestions and criticism, while David Marquand offered some very good last-minute refinements. My thanks to them all, never forgetting my father, who came up with the most important suggestion of all – the title.

A book written this quickly requires a very flexible editorial infrastructure, and more thanks to Caroline Michel, my editor at Vintage, for providing it. It was her gentle persistence that finally persuaded me to take the plunge and write again, and she has proved resourceful, helpfully critical and calm throughout. Liz Cowen was a considerable copy-editor operating under intense pressure, and my personal assistant at the *Observer*, Angela Burton, must be heartily sick of the photocopier and dispatch rider. Thanks to you both.

It's 3.30 a.m., and there's much more to do yet – along with another day at the *Observer*. I hope I've included all my thank yous and not inadvertently left anybody out – certainly not Jane and the children. These books couldn't have been written without all your forbearance and affection. Thanks hugely. And I hope you the reader, the most important person of all, enjoy the result.

Will Hutton, March 1997

1

The Strange Rebirth of Liberal England

The British are favoured. We are a governable people who have enjoyed and expect to continue to enjoy civil peace and rising living standards. We have won our wars. The genocides, hyperinflations and revolutions which have destabilised other national communities have not visited our shores. At the end of the twentieth century we still remain in the first rank of nations, even if not where we once stood.

And for a very old country there is life in us yet. The flair of our designers, the exuberance of our popular music and our strength in industries as disparate as accountancy and the manufacture of Formula One cars are all tribute to a continuing native genius. Some of our older industrial cities have managed, against the odds, to throw off the long legacy of decline. There are strong and growing social movements insisting that the degradation of the environment cannot continue. British women are entering work in unparalleled numbers and bringing with them a new creativity and commitment. We demand of ourselves ever higher standards. We are aware of enlarging choices and possibilities fed by the new technologies and the opening up of the globe.

Yet at this moment when the future is so pregnant with possibility, the Conservative party and the body of ideas that has succoured it over its long years in power paradoxically insist that we can do nothing together that might improve our circumstances and exploit the signs of this vitality – or at least nothing that does not correspond to their very particular brand of individualism. We have no choice but to obey the injunctions of the genre of market capitalism they have developed over the last eighteen years and to which we owe every and any improvement about us. Our public institutions, if they cannot be privatised, must be made to ape those in the private sector. To entertain the reform of our political system, as John Major has said before the general election, is to put in peril a thousand years of history. Our future is Conservative as mapped by the decades of Thatcherism and its bastard child, Majorism.

This is an extraordinary claim. It supposes that the present is unimprovable, or defective only to the extent that the rule of one form of market capitalism has not been sufficiently extended. Solutions to any problem lie in asserting more individualism and averting as far as possible any development of public institutions or public initiative. That would involve public expenditure and, worse, taxation. To tax has become the sin above any other, even though eighteen years of Conservatism have produced a rise in the proportion of taxation raised as a proportion of national output,[1] while redistributing it so that more is shouldered by those on average and below-average incomes and less by those on higher incomes.

Nor is it admissible to regulate private business. The Conservatives themselves may have been compelled to set up agencies that regulate the privatised utilities and financial services industries, but this is seen as a regrettable concession which should be reversed when politically possible and as the industries mature. Regulation implies the direction of private conduct in ways that might not be chosen voluntarily. Even if it has wider benefits, it still implies an intervention in the free actions of companies. And this conception of freedom – or more accurately the freedom of contract – is the heart of the matter. As we will explore in Chapter 2, the Conservatives believe that the route to economic and social efficiency lies in insisting upon the primacy of permanently renegotiable contract relationships whoever you are: a GP and a hospital, a firm and its suppliers. Forget any imbalance of power, of knowledge, of financial muscle, or of wider social consequences which make contracting unstable and inefficient. Contract is King.

But the extravagant claims made for the results of all this free contracting – from the financial system to the National Health Service – do not bear close scrutiny. Britain has grown less rapidly and the gains from the lower growth are bitterly unequally distributed. The scope for the abuse of British democracy, ever present in a country without a written constitution, has become more evident as the transformation of the public sector into a web of contract relationships has been prosecuted with little care for accountability and transparency. A new value system has grown up in which everything can have a price put on its head and is potentially up for sale. Concepts which a civilised community holds dear – the ethic of care in medicine, of justice in the courts, of service in the public sector – have been threatened by the overarching ethic that they must be on the market, even though, as Bob Kuttner argues, society could never allow them to go bust.[2] Sporting excellence and artistic achievement are similarly threatened. There must be another way; and if there is not we must invent one.

Such a plea is not made carelessly. We have learnt more about other market economies and societies as the world has become smaller, and what is evident is not the homogeneity of their cultures and organisation, but their heterogeneity. As choices widen for us as individuals, we are simultaneously told that there are no choices about how we organise ourselves collectively. That we can have no other institutions and practices but those we have inherited or had imposed upon us by the simplistic verities of Conservative rule. Such propositions are neither reasonable nor democratic. Of course there are choices about the kind of capitalist society we want to become, about the balance we want to strike between market efficiencies and social justice and about how we organise our democracy. No veto is placed upon our freely expressed will by globalisation, as some on the Conservative right argue; in truth the new world, if properly interpreted, empowers us all the more.

Moreover, the capacity to make such choices is at the heart of democracy. To win elections and to initiate change through legislation is the precept upon which democracy is built. The notion is inadmissible that the only use to which public power can be put is to make the world safe for a free enterprise which does not accept social responsibilities and which tries to place risk firmly on individuals rather than acknowledge that the role of government is to organise its fair distribution. It is also, as I will argue later, amoral.

One lesson of our times may be that capitalism has triumphed for the moment in the great battle with socialism – if socialism is understood to mean a planned economy, extensive public ownership, negligible private property rights and a directed society, in which political and civil liberties are not entrenched in law. It was right that it should win, even if many socialists would say that such a description of their aims traduces what they ever stood for or intended. But the moral and religious values which informed the socialist and social democratic movements of the twentieth century, along with their fierce advocacy of liberty, cannot be consigned to history without endangering the civilisation which we prize. Another lesson of our times is surely that the operation of the unchecked market, whatever its success in sending effective messages about what is scarce and what is abundant, has an inherent tendency to produce unreasonable inequality, economic instability and immense concentrations of private, unaccountable power. To protect itself, society has to have countervailing powers built into the operation of the market, otherwise the market cannot deliver its promise. Instead it collapses into licence masquerading as liberty, spivvery dressed up as risk-taking and exploitation in the guise of efficiency and flexibility.

Thus the challenge at the turn of the century is to learn from past mistakes on both sides of the political divide. Capitalism has won, certainly, but that does not mean that societies cannot shape it to meet their wider goals. Different ethical values apart from the market ethic must be protected; and trust, fairness and the acceptance of obligations should not be seen as tiresome obstacles in the creation of economic efficiency, but as central to it. Human values need to be incorporated into the core of market processes not merely to produce a kinder, more tolerable society – fundamental though that is – but a well-functioning market economy. This is the core of the stakeholding concept. But to accept the need for change, there first has to be acceptance that the current system is not working well, to dispute, in short, Conservative claims about the nature and scale of their achievement. It is to those that we now turn.

The State We're In Now

In the Conservative lexicon Britain is an unparalleled success – the enterprise centre of Europe, with a dynamic economy generating employment to a degree which is the envy of the European Union. A more honest appraisal is more sober.

The economy may now be growing, but the long-run growth rate has weakened. Over-reliant on personal consumption to propel the economy, which is still higher proportionally than in other leading industrialised countries, the sustainable growth rate cannot rise until investment rises. But public investment is reaching new postwar lows, even allowing for the reductions accompanying privatisation, while private investment remains depressed and lifeless. Manufacturing investment is falling calamitously. Too much private investment is dependent upon foreign multinationals, for even here there are problems. Britain's 'success' in attracting inward foreign direct investment is trumpeted from the rooftops, but every pound of investment that entered Britain between 1991 and 1995 was on average trumped by half as much again leaving the country in British direct investment overseas.[3] Inflation, although low by British standards, is still high in comparison with other leading industrialised countries; and with a recovery so reliant on credit, rising property prices and consumption the risk of its re-emergence is ever present. Earnings, for example, are already rising at some 5 per cent.

Inequality is at record postwar levels, with the incomes of those at the bottom, after housing costs, falling in real terms, as the disadvantaged alternate between periods of insecure, low-paid employment and income support, while the incomes of those at the top continue to balloon. Although the numbers officially unemployed have fallen below two million, nearly another two and half million more men and women stand idly in the wings, wanting work, but not claiming the benefit that categorises them as formally unemployed.[4] Job insecurity for men is rising sharply, and a majority are now compelled to retire prematurely before the age of sixty-five. The number of poor children has risen from 1.4 million in 1961, the *Family Income Expenditure Survey* estimates, to 3.8 million in 1991 – around a third of all children. Another survey reports that only 4 per cent of boys and 3 per cent of girls who were placed in care at any time or lived in a family facing financial difficulties went on to education at degree level – compared to 13 per cent of boys and 14 per cent of girls without those handicaps in their childhood years.[5] Inequality has become deeply embedded.

Indeed, the rise in inequality has gone deep into the British social and psychological make-up with very little comment. Inequality helps to make the economy more unstable and the distribution of incomes more unfair, but that is only the beginning. It is inequality that fuels short-termism as the quest for ever higher incomes becomes more intense and feverish. It is inequality that feeds the new insecurity as the penalty in lost income for any move down the job hierarchy grows more severe. It is inequality that makes those at the bottom feel ever more desperate about their condition as the prospects of joining even those on average incomes seem ever more remote. And it is that which leads them to turn in on themselves, to take more and more dangerous drugs, thereby helping to drive the rise in crime. Inequality is perhaps the single most salient fact in contemporary British society.

The roll-back of the state in the name of deregulation and privatisation has apparently brought efficiency gains through aggressive rounds of lay-offs and redundancies, but the gains have proved to be transient. Privatised bus services, for example, have meant ageing buses, rising fares and unco-ordinated timetables. The regulator of independent TV companies complains that the quality of programmes is falling in the quest for larger audiences on small budgets. There are inexplicable power cuts, water shortages and train cancellations.

Rounds of takeovers and mergers have brought forth new concentrations of private monopoly power. Three companies dominate the deregulated bus industry; three companies dominate the partially deregulated world of independent television; and the same phenomenon is emerging among privatised utilities. More than half the regional electricity companies have been taken over by American utilities with a poor record of meeting regulatory and environmental standards at home. In place of public monopolies we now have private and foreign-owned monopolies, whose lines of accountability – given British company law – are pitifully weak and whose regulatory structures are poor.

Buoyed up by 'success' in the economic domain, the new Conservatives have sought to extend into social life the same individualism, market-contract dominance and competition which have underpinned their economic reforms. Hospitals have to make financial returns on their assets without the freedom to invest; courts charge for divorce proceedings in order to move to self-sufficiency. Schools compete for children, university research departments for research funds. There is no corner of these islands where the new writ, in one form or another, does not run. Justice, medicine, and university research subordinate the values that animate their practice to that of market contract. The merits are contestable at best, at worst downright perverse.

And the attempt to rebase the country's economic and social organisation around a new individualism does not stop at that. Criminal activity is held to be the individual's responsibility and wider economic and social circumstances are dismissed or downplayed as a cause of crime. Crime is portrayed increasingly as an individualist act to which the proper response is not individual rehabilitation but individual punishment. If there are wider forces at work, then Conservatives choose to see them as originating not as the consequences of poverty and inequality but as the by-products of government and the welfare state – unintended perhaps, but unmistakable none the less. Tax incentives make it advantageous not to marry. Income support makes it attractive for teenage girls to have babies. Family breakdown, complex in its causes, is simplified into a story of the bad state and the individual corrupted by its influences. Two events which recently horrified the nation – the stabbing of Philip Lawrence and the murder of James Bulger – have been turned into morality plays in which lack of individual responsibility, soft sentencing and poor morals have been seen as central. There is some truth in the complaint; what is disturbing is how it has crowded out any other explanation of deviant behaviour.

Indeed, as evidence of social fragmentation mounts, there is an increasingly shrill cry to remoralise society – in which morality is regarded as the prohibition of individual actions backed by repressive legislation. Economic and social reforms, which might address the roots of these problems, are seen as a return to what has failed; instead the future is one of moral individuals, caned at school, smacked at home and wary of steep punishment in prison fixed by automatic sentencing, who keep their families together and so stand as bulwarks against social implosion. The march to the deregulated hyper-efficient market economy – the enterprise centre of Europe – can thus continue, immune to the social consequences.

Nor does the talk of admonition and prohibition stop there. The climate which produces constraints and bans does not begin and end with school expulsions and longer sentences for offenders of all ages; it extends seamlessly into the censorship of books, films and theatre. A prison ship docks in Portland Harbour to house the overflow of prisoners. The social security system becomes ever more punitive. It is this new Conservative culture that produced the extraordinary Police Bill, which in its original form gave police constables the right to bug the offices of anybody they considered predisposed towards or perhaps knowing about criminal activity without any prior authorisation. An Orwellian Big Brother of the right, not the left, looms. Some initiatives can be justified as ways of strengthening the wider social architecture – too easy divorce, for example, to the extent that it encourages family breakdown with heavy psychological costs for children, should be limited. But without parallel moves to attack the well-springs of the forces atomising society and destroying the networks of social sanction which lie at the root of any well-ordered community, many current 'reforms' are exposed as little more than vengeful repression. With no bill of rights, entrenched liberties, or formal separation of the judiciary from the executive and legislative branches of government, long-standing British freedoms are now actively under threat.

The Ideology Behind It All

All this is serious enough, but perhaps more serious is the manner in which it has been done. For as each year has passed and the drive to install the market principle has reached ever more distant borders, so what began as a reasoned attack on over-powerful and obstructive trade unions and inefficient public ownership has hardened into an ideology as pernicious, in its way, as communism. The vocabulary of Western liberalism – of freedom, choice, independence and even morality – has been captured and recast into thought categories consistent only with competitive economic individualism. Freedom is defined as the freedom to buy and sell; choice as the right to exercise choice in markets; independence is independence from the state; moral conduct is the exercise of individual choice.

With the words programmed to have these meanings, any questions that use them have their answers prefigured. Thus enlarging freedom means enlarging economic freedom; maximising choice means maximising the operation of markets. No public institution can be independent because, of necessity, it is government-owned and financed and the state is collectivist; to be independent therefore implies that an institution be private. An independent university, for example, in this vocabulary is impossible, unless it is a private university.

This language is but the first step in the construction of a sealed thought process impregnable to criticism or evidence from the real world. The great achievement of classical economics has been to demonstrate that, under highly artificial assumptions, the act of freely buying and selling in markets in response to price signals produces a perfect economic outcome. This result cannot be improved upon, because if it could somebody would still be buying or selling; in other words the rules of the games have been drawn up to deliver the required result. In the abstract it is an elegant system; it bears little relation to reality.

Indeed, the theory is absurd as we shall explore later; few markets could ever hope to meet its restrictive assumptions, and its power of comprehending real life situations is indicative at best, wholly wrong at worst. Yet it is very attractive as a defence of capitalism, and neatly makes the case against the state and forms of public intervention; for if this is the natural tendency of capitalism, then the only reason why it does not behave in this way is because it has been obstructed; and those obstructions cannot come from the market itself, but from external obstacles put in its way. And those obstacles are initiated only by government.

Thus the absurdities and tautologies of the theory matter little to a business class irritated by taxation, which regards any obstruction to its aims and ambitions as irksome. For a Rupert Murdoch or a Lord Hanson to have at hand an explanation of the world which lionises their efforts while demonising those of government could hardly be more congenial; better still it is a justification for minimising the exposure of their profits to tax and protecting their companies from public intervention. What they do is best; what governments do is worst.

Indeed, so congenial is the theory that no effort is spared to prove its success. Economies that are not organised exactly according to its precepts are dismissed as sclerotic no-hopers. Germany, mired in the business of re-unification and suffering until recently from an overvalued currency, is in the economic doldrums, but British accounts rarely mention either factor in explaining its problems. In Conservative eyes it is just not free market enough, even though it has twice as much investment per man as Britain, its productivity is higher and it runs a massive trade surplus. Properly adjusted for the numbers of unemployed who are excluded by official British measures, even the unemployment record of the two countries is broadly comparable, with Germany's worsened by near recession conditions and Britain's flattered by five years of recovery. In Britain, for example, 19·3 per cent of households were workless in 1994, the latest year for which there are comparable figures; in Germany the figure stood at 15·5 per cent. Yet, judging by most British assessments, it cannot be long before Germany – twice the size of the British economy – declares unconditional surrender to superior British free-market economic forces.

And if the present is viewed through the distorting mirror of ideology, an increasing effort is being made to re-interpret the past. The part played by the Conservative party in running down the Empire, building the welfare state and sustaining the postwar alliance with the United States is now portrayed as betrayal:[6] the welfare state was always too expensive and to ally with the United States while giving up Empire was a supine acceptance of a secondary role. It all should have been resisted. In particular a new history is being invented in which Conservative politicians who argued for British membership of the European Community in the 1960s and 1970s are depicted as lying Quislings, who deliberately hid the long-term aim of Europe's founding fathers – to build a politically integrated Europe – from the British people. The former Prime Minister, Ted Heath, is a particular *bête noire* even if, as he protests, he never disguised the political implications of British membership of the European Union.

In sum, the right has developed its own ideological thought structure. Although it likes to mock liberal opinion for 'political correctness', there is a parallel political correctness of the right. It has a vocabulary; a determist economic theory; and a history with its own heroes and villains. But above all it has an idea of sovereignty, bound up with the centrality of the House of Commons in British life, which has reached iconic ideological status.

The celebration of the sovereignty of the House of Commons, along with the constitution and the voting system in which it is embedded, has steadily moved up the pecking order of the Conservative right's ideological thought structure. The fusion of the executive and legislature has been central to the Thatcherite experiment in order to legislate for the new 'freedoms', although the Conservatives have never won a majority of the votes cast in any British election. As the result of the reforms has been to weaken many of the intermediate institutions in British society, notably local government, the House of Commons has assumed yet more importance as the political forum of the nation, and has been a pliable instrument in organising ever more repressive legislation as crime and social disorder have climbed. The British parliamentary system has been essential to the Conservative project.

To this important attribute another must now be added: that the House of Commons, as the cockpit of the nation, which has been under Conservative control for most of this century, represents an idea of Britishness that is happily congruent with Conservatism. It is a clubbable place whose debating procedures follow closely those of the Oxford and Cambridge Unions. The formal lines of accountability are so haphazard that much of ministers' authority relies on the sense that chaps like them can be trusted. And in Britain the accent and deportment of the privately educated – of whom many more are Conservative – are a solid guarantor of trust. The background and attitude of Conservative MPs naturally attract them to a system in which they feel more at ease and whose demands sit more happily with their attributes.

But what sharpens this loyalty is the belief that parliament is now under mortal threat from the ambitions of mainland Europeans to construct a more integrated Europe, necessarily transferring sovereignty to Brussels. The threat from overseas only helps to harden the sense that the House of Commons, complete with its first-past-the-post voting system and centralisation of authority in London, must be defended to the last. National identity and the interests of the Conservative party neatly coincide. The sovereignty of the House of Commons, free market economics and an increasingly vocal Euroscepticism are thus profoundly interconnected and interdependent. Together they constitute the New Conservative ideology.

The Decline and Fall of Conservative England

This position is shot through with inconsistencies. The business and financial élite may find that a philosophy which so happily underwrites their own interests has unrefusable attractions, but its application across the gamut of the economy and society has unleashed such powerful destabilising influences that their own economic and social interests are directly threatened. It is also untenable to argue for cosmopolitan, internationalist free trade and the inability to resist market forces, while at the same time insisting that the sovereignty of the House of Commons be defended to the last to allow independent national action. A philosophy which positively welcomes inward investment and foreign ownership of British assets – because ownership is said not to matter – cannot at the same time damn European integration because it threatens sovereignty.

The cumulative impact of the large flows of inward direct investment is to will away the real sovereignty of government over the economy, even as there are ever louder protests about political sovereignty being ceded to Brussels – which paradoxically would give British governments more rather than less power in relation to multinationals. Indeed, the multinationals themselves have their own political agenda; they are explicitly for the Single Market, British membership of the European Union and even the single currency, in sum the basis for their prosperous operation from Britain. The dilemma was highlighted when Toyota, whose investment in Britain is regarded as tribute to the success of Conservative economic and social policies, said in February, before the general election, that new investment in Britain would be jeopardised if we refused to join the single currency. Free market capitalism, in which the movement of capital is free, is not consistent with powerful, independent sovereign nation states.

This fundamental incoherence is now at the bottom of the Conservative party's disintegration. It is appropriate that Europe is the epicentre of its problems, but that only dramatises fissures and inconsistencies which run much deeper. The Conservative party, advocate of the organic growth of institutions, is married to a philosophy that produces the most revolutionary and detraditionalising forces of all. The market principle, whether it is undermining bus services or degrading television, is one of which Conservatism should be suspicious.

Its difficulty is that the same principle justifies extravagant salaries in the City, low marginal tax rates and anti-union legislation. But the wider political problem is that against every investment banker hymning market forces after another deal can be set a small shop-keeper driven out of business by a supermarket chain.

Nor is that all. Rising inequality, as we will explore in Chapter 2, is itself a source of economic instability, creating uneven patterns of demand that are problematic for the business community. Indeed, as the businessmen who signed the Institute of Public Policy Research's report, *Promoting Prosperity*,[7] put it, the gains from further rounds of market liberalisation are being progressively exhausted. Employers do not need to be further empowered against organised labour; what they now need is a steady supply of better educated and skilled workers. In the run-up to the general election the CBI, extraordinarily, protested that anti-union legislation outlawing public sector strikes was unworkable.

Thus an important element of Conservative support finds it can no longer wholeheartedly back its party as it has in the past. If over most of this century British business has unthinkingly offered the party its support because Labourism purported to be the enemy of free enterprise, that equation has now changed. In part this is the result of a hard-headed assessment of who will win the election; and in part recognition that Labour has genuinely dropped many of the policies which business has found historically alarming and embraced those that they favour. After all, businessmen can see that there is a panoply of areas, from improved transport to the proper regulation of personal pensions, which require more determined rules, surveillance and active intervention if they are to prosper. This is not part of contemporary Conservatism's game plan.

But if that is one fissure, another is the argument over centralisation. The paradox of Thatcherism/Majorism is now well known: that a strong state has been required to impose market freedoms and a wider individualism, taking to new extremes the centralising tendency built-in into the British state which has been obvious since 1945. But again this runs against the grain, not merely of a long-standing localist tradition in British culture, but of a Conservatism that sees in the 'small platoons' of society its very bedrock, taking its cue from Edmund Burke. One author, Simon Jenkins of *The Times*, has gone so far as to dub the process the nationalisation of Britain. The concentration of power in central government's hands has been remarkable; but what gives especial cause for complaint has been the failure to incorporate systems of accountability or to ensure that public spending is allocated fairly.

In education, for example, the Funding Agency for Schools – a centralised quango whose board is unrepresentatively packed with active or sympathetic Conservatives[8] – directs moneys to grant-maintained schools that are significantly more generous than the allocations to their local authority counterparts. Similarly, the government caps spending in different local authorities, so that superimposed on one layer of inequity lies another, felt acutely when the resulting budgets are so tight that they force painful choices about closures and teacher redundancies. Protests in counties like Shropshire and Somerset have forced the government partially to rescind its rate-capping orders, but the damage has been done. Across the country there is a sense of grievance that decisions about funding which should be taken locally are being removed from local hands, and that the drive to grant-maintained schools should override local preferences.

Education is not alone. The same story in essence could be told of housing, of compulsory competitive tendering, of planning appeals, of policing, or of health. In urban areas where Labour control is more or less taken for granted, the government has been careless of the reaction; but as heartland English Conservative counties have been affected by the same initiatives, local Conservative élites have begun to protest at the attack on their competence and authority. Here again the party has divided its own support, making it harder to sustain the hold on 'Middle England' of which it boasts.

And to these haemorrhages of support can be added another: the first signs of a revolt against law and order legislation that withdraws important civil liberties. As the Police

Bill proceeded through parliament, it became clear that limits of tolerance were being reached. Twenty-nine Conservative Peers voted for an Opposition amendment requiring that police bugging be authorised in advance by a commissioner, which although short of the proper safeguard of judicial authorisation and containing important let-out clauses, was an improvement on the original clause. Crucially the government did not dare to reverse the amendment in the Commons, as an array of Conservative columnists and leader writers, civil liberty campaigners, barristers and law lords made their opposition clear – along with the *Observer*. Liberal England, whose voice has been stilled for nigh on twenty years, is beginning to stir.

But if Middle England and business are expressing ever greater reserve about the mix of more individualism and the centralising state, the appeal to Euroscepticism as a potential re-unifying pole around which Conservative forces can group is no less divisive. For the logic of the Eurosceptic position is withdrawal from the European Union – a step that threatens not just inward investment, which is a pillar of Conservative economic policy, but more importantly the direct economic interests of part of the City and some British multinational companies like BP and Unilever. Anti-Brussels feelings are strong among high Tories and the New Right alike, but there is a pragmatic Conservative tradition which is profoundly uneasy about the undertone of xenophobia – and the consequences for the British state of being outside the inner councils of Europe or its markets, in a wider world where regional political and economic blocs could become more, not less, significant. They also genuinely believe in European integration. A rallying cry that divides your own support and threatens some of your core constituency's own interests is definitionally self-defeating.

Conservative Britain, and Conservative England in particular, are on the wane. Yet even while their fortunes decline and the appetite for a change of direction mounts, the momentum of Conservative ideas and their dominance over national debate continues curiously unabated. Government is distrusted. Taxation is regarded as an evil, to be evaded, avoided and reduced. Crime is portrayed as an individual act. Divorce is blamed on an easy approach to morality and selfishness towards children. The single-parent family is accused of being an important source of social disintegration. The cane, smacking and corporal punishment are advocated as necessary means of child control and instilling discipline. Euroscepticism is more powerful than Euro-enthusiasm. And so on.

Thus while the results of the current mix of policies are increasingly deplored, alternative intellectual and political trends have nothing like the power of the still ascendant right – and could be snuffed out. New Labour has won support partly because of the electorate's sheer weariness with a party that has governed for so long, and partly because it has attempted to reshape its policies within the prevailing Conservative ethos – while preserving as far as it can its own historic objectives. So far it has been a successful strategy.

But it is dangerous, too. For the current position is unstable. Unless an ascendant body of ideas can be assembled, underpinned by a political philosophy that incorporates a different worldview and policy direction, Labour will find in office that it governs in essence as a nicer group of Conservatives. This will legitimise the right and so encourage it to move further to the right, even as Labour's own political position becomes more threadbare. Worse, given the scale and nature of Britain's economic and social problems, the risks of failure are high.

All, however, is not lost. Even the constrained Labour party has kept a minimalist position which could set in train a powerful dynamic for change. It is committed to important reforms of British democracy which address many of the problems over centralisation and lack of accountability. It wishes to reshape British capitalism – a little. It is determined to lower long-term unemployment. The mere fact of its election will help to recapture the vocabulary of Western liberalism from the right. At an important moment in our national affairs, it is appropriate that it should now win office – and win decisively.

The task ahead is to extend the critique of the way the economy and society has been run, and from that basis to offer a more robust framework in which a non-Conservative party can govern. The process of intellectual fightback has to be accelerated. The Conservative right are wrong. Their mistakes must be demonstrated – and they must be compelled to rethink, rather as the left has had to over the last eighteen years. Only then will British democracy and civil society be safe. It is a rich and important prize – as important as winning a parliamentary majority.

2

WHY MARKETS GO WRONG

YOU'RE IN YOUR car, it's the morning rush-hour and you're in a hurry – there never seems to be enough time. The traffic is heavy, and suddenly it comes to a halt. A bus ahead is standing still at the bus stop as passengers board, and each one has to show their pass or buy a ticket from the driver. There is no conductor, so this takes two or three minutes, especially when it's busy. The tail-back behind the bus snakes back, jamming up the intersections. It's a frustrating nightmare; you would prefer to travel by bus or train, rather than by car, but the service is not comfortable, quick or reliable. It can't be long, you think, before the whole road network collapses into gridlock.

It's a familiar enough experience – and a classic legacy of the Conservative years. The bus operator, after all, by stripping out two-man crews is making his buses more efficient. Why pay a wage to a conductor when the driver can take the money for tickets? But the efficiency for the bus operator has inefficient consequences for the rest of us. It slows up the bus, and provokes slower traffic flows. The sacked bus conductor is added to the pool of the unemployed, and so social security payments are increased, crowding out the public expenditure that might otherwise have been allocated to improving the road or rail network. The next job he will obtain will, as typically for most of the unemployed, be lower paid and have fewer employment rights. His life and that of his family will have been blighted.

Moreover, one small element in the fabric of society that

helps to regulate social life and act as a social sanction has disappeared. The bus conductor offers a reassurance to travellers that there will be no threat from rowdy or violent passengers which a lone driver cannot match; if, for example, some young teenagers take drugs on the bus or act threateningly, the conductor is on hand as both witness and steward. His or her very presence acts as a prior sanction; here is the representative not just of authority but of wider society. Once his or her job has gone, and new, poor codes of behaviour become commonplace on buses, another small chink in our armoury against the descent into civic barbarism is removed.

Nor is that all. The bus, very probably, is carrying the livery not of the old bus service but of a new private operator and is one of many that clutter up the road. Over the last ten years the 'state', in the guise of municipal and county bus services, has been rolled back to be replaced by private bus operators in a new, deregulated bus market. The rationale is familiar: private is best and competition is the best spur to efficiency. Yet the results have not been quite as predicted. Because the capital and running costs of buses cannot be altered – after all, a bus is a bus with wheels and an engine and a route is a route – the 'efficiency gains' can only come from four sources: allowing the bus fleet to age; cutting wages and wider employment costs, such as employers' pension contributions; cutting out unprofitable routes; and putting up fares. And so, as mentioned briefly in Chapter 1, it has come to pass. Britain's buses are older and more prone to breakdown; staffing has been lowered, wages cut and social overheads pared down; and the service at quieter times of the day and to outlying districts has been reduced.

Moreover, the many new private bus companies have been culled by a relentless process of takeover and merger. Those operators with stock market quotations have issued shares to raise cash to buy up their competitors, usually after a period in which they have used their superior financial muscle to compete them into submission. Stagecoach, one such operator, has had over twenty references to the Monopolies and Mergers Commission over its competitive strategies, but along with two other companies now accounts for over 50 per cent of bus traffic in Britain.[1] A local public monopoly has been replaced by bigger private monopolists, able to raise fares as they choose, and so lift profits to justify their high share prices, which they need to raise more cash from the stock market. Passenger numbers, at the receiving end of this process, not surprisingly have fallen. And environmentally, village life is even more dependent upon the car – one more twist in the desertification of our countryside.[2]

However, from the Conservative point of view, we have to live with all these consequences. If the private bus operator considers two-man buses inefficient, then he must cut out conductors; it is inadmissible for the state to interfere with how he wants to arrange his business. The contract between bus operator and shareholders demands that profits be maximised, and services reduced. The passengers' view on the mix of fares, the range of services and staffing on buses is irrelevant; it can be expressed only through the market. And if taxpayers might have gained from maintaining the old system as citizens and passengers, even if it involved subsidy, that too does not matter; a different judgement has been made by our masters and that is what counts. Tax cuts are an over-riding priority, and reducing any form of public activity a moral imperative. The wise society with proper democratic mechanisms would take a more rounded view of what constitutes efficiency and make a more pragmatic judgement about the balance between private and public interests, but in the Conservative universe that is not possible. It would offend the primacy of contract; overturn the drive towards individualism; and demand a recasting of the way democracy is practised. Traffic gridlock and another contribution to social disintegration result.

That, in microcosm, is the heart of the criticism against the way in which contemporary British capitalism has been allowed to develop. Efficiency is a much more complex notion than simple cost minimisation seen through the eyes of the managers of any given enterprise. The balance sheet of gains and losses is much wider than a simple calculus of one firm's profitability; the effects of actions in one sphere spill over into another and have a subsequent impact not merely on the economy, but also on society, that can be undesirable. We, as a community, must be able to act to change matters if we choose.

It is not reasonable to argue that these are the consequences of actions in free markets, which will regulate themselves, and that they represent some overarching economic logic independent of institutions and culture which cannot be changed or challenged; market actions are shaped by institutions and cultures. There are important questions of how we want to balance public and private interests – and how we want to distribute income, and in a more fundamental sense, risk. Governments, any more than societies, cannot shrug their shoulders and walk away from these issues, pleading that markets produce the best outcomes, that individualism is the only philosophic cornerstone around which to conceptualise human action and that public action always delivers perversely wrong results. Such claims do not stand up.

The example of buses dramatises all those points. The emergence of new private bus monopolists could not have happened but for Britain's easy-going approach to unfair competition and the way in which the stock exchange facilitates predatory takeover. These are not inevitable features of a market economy; they are peculiar to Britain. Equally the privatisation of bus services has knock-on economic consequences; as bus fleets age, so new orders for buses slow. Local labour markets are affected by the increase in unemployment. Social security spending rises.

But there are second-round effects on society. Social integration, family life and community, as we have argued already, are all diminished. Workers in the bus industry realise that their jobs are more insecure, and that their employers are compelled to be increasingly aggressive about employment; that affects in turn their loyalty to the company and the value they place in upgrading their skills. Why bother if you could be laid off next week? Insecurity is one more incentive not to acquire skills and hastens the arrival of a low-wage, low-skill Britain.

Then there is the question of how equitably risk is distributed in these conditions. As labour regulations are weakened and trade union power reduced, workers are less capable of protecting themselves from redundancy in the bus industry, as elsewhere – they are more at risk of income loss and periods of unemployment. Now in one sense this is an obvious side-effect of a functioning labour market. If the market works well any displaced workers can presumably be more easily hired by other firms. But, on the other hand, the degree of risk has increased – and has been displaced on to individuals with necessarily lower savings and weaker chances of being re-employed than more highly educated and wealthy managers. The outrage about 'fat cats' is not just fed by jealousy; it is a real action to the injustice of an unfair allocation of risk and reward.

This is doubly enforced if the whole network of support structures is weakened. Unskilled low wage-earners, definitionally those most at risk, plainly find it financially harder to provide for themselves than those with higher incomes; private insurance for health or a pension in old age requires a steady flow of premiums which such workers find it difficult to maintain. The National Health Service, a sound public education system, unemployment insurance and a reasonable old age pension are not add-ons; they are essential mechanisms which help individuals to deal with high systemic levels of risk.

The Conservative focus on a narrow, book-keeper's conception of efficiency neglects all these spillover dynamics in our economy and society, relying instead on the supposedly self-regulating properties of markets to correct those adverse trends. It is reluctant to accept any kind of moral verdict on the inequitable patterns of risk and income that result, any obligation to influence firm and market behaviour through amending the pattern of incentives, legal and regulatory requirements of wider institutional patterns, and any need to sustain a high standard of universal collective insurance through the welfare state, a minimum safety net apart. As a result, the effects of changes in the bus industry and hundreds like it, ricocheting around our economy and society, are going unchallenged and unshaped. This chapter could have begun with an account of the BSE and E-Coli crises, linking the pressure to deliver ever higher financial returns in the abattoir industry with a lax approach to regulation which has delivered a public health scandal; or it could have discussed how personal pensions have been mis-sold in their millions and how feeble the redress has been, with the numbers compensated in their thousands. Either story would have been a good vehicle to show how the results of apparent efficiency between two contracting parties – to process meat and to provide personal pensions – have malign spillover effects on the rest of the economy and society which we cannot ignore.

To object to these processes is not to argue that by contrast firms should remain frozen in aspic, every job is a job for life and every last detail of market actions requires to be regulated; a market economy that was not constantly changing and reorganising the patterns of production and work would not be working effectively – and it needs its freedoms. The question is how to build a capitalist structure that can regulate itself better. It is how society should account for the wider costs of individual actions, how the resulting risks could be distributed fairly and how they should be insured against and paid for.

For over the years, if these questions are not answered satisfactorily, both the economy and society are corroded. In the same way that individualism and free contracting do not spontaneously produce the best outcome in organising local bus networks, the sale of personal pensions or the processing of meat, so they are also poor at delivering a high wage, high investing, innovative economy and a fair, well-ordered society. The next step in the argument is to try and understand why. It might seem difficult in parts – but bear with me. It is central to our lives and our political choices.

Why Contracting Gets in a Fix

Why does the market not have the powerful self-regulating properties that theorists suggest it should possess? If these properties were present market economies would not alternate between boom and bust. There would be some stable level of inequality, because as the incomes of those at the top rose so more and more people would want to acquire the skills that made them rich, and the supply of newcomers would drive down the incomes of those at the top. The trend towards monopoly would be weakened because new entrants into markets would displace the old monopolists. There would be no under-investment and short-terminism because long-sighted financiers would expect to make high profits from plugging the gaps. We would live in a land of milk and honey; that we don't suggests something is wrong.

At the centre of the market system is the contract between two parties: one buys; one sells. Capitalism can thus be envisioned purely as a network of contracts mediated by price, indeed that is exactly how free-market economists portray it. Employers hire workers for a price – their wage. Companies hire land and offices for a rent. They borrow money at a rate of interest. They contract to deliver goods for a price. And so on. To say that something is amiss with the process of market self-regulation is to say that this system of contracting has an innate tendency to go wrong.

Perhaps the best place to begin the quest to explain the shortcomings of market contracting is the financial markets. In many respects these most perfectly possess the preconditions for successful 'contract market' outcomes. The prices of financial assets in today's markets reflect many buying and selling decisions, so it is very rare, indeed almost impossible for any one buyer or seller to corner the market; the distorting force of monopoly is almost entirely absent. And the buyers and sellers are remarkably well informed and driven by the desire to maximise profits; after all, information is instantaneously disseminated on tens of thousands of dealing screens and nobody in the financial markets need feel that bonds of loyalty or any higher ethic should obstruct the over-riding injunction – make money. If there is one set of markets that could be relied upon to get its judgements broadly right, it is this.

Yet, as Keynes observed in the 1930s, and more recently the famous financial speculator turned political economist George Soros has reconfirmed, financial markets are very unstable. Soros has made his billions because financial markets fail. They overshoot; they get stuck with valuations that are too high or too low and which can remain in place for months and even years. In the early 1930s Keynes observed that even very low interest rates could not persuade investors to borrow: partly because they had no use for the money in a very depressed economy and partly because they thought interest rates might go even lower – or not budge at all; either way they had no reason to do anything. Keynes described the condition as a 'liquidity trap'. Something very similar has happened over the last few years in Japan. Equally in the foreign exchange markets the dollar, pound, mark and yen have all recently gone through periods of systematic under- or over-valuation which have lasted months and even years.

The puzzle is why this should be so, for if this happens in the near-perfect conditions of the financial markets, the same problems will highlight themselves even more emphatically in the markets for goods, services, houses and labour which are more imperfect – and the public sector into which the contract principle has been driven by successive Conservative governments. Soros's theory, outlined in his *Alchemy of Finance*[3] and repeated more recently in an article for the *Atlantic Monthly*[4] is very simple; prices cannot do the job of driving markets to settled points of balance because they themselves are part of the buying and selling decisions that they are supposedly co-ordinating. Prices are, he says, 'reflexive' – and their very reflexivity creates an unstable dynamic. This is even more marked in the financial markets, where contracts can be bought and sold in such enormous size and with such immediacy.

So what is reflexivity? It may seem complex and opaque, but in truth the idea is disarmingly simple. We all know that we behave differently if we are watched; we complain that we could get our first service in at tennis, for example, or balance a ball on our head if there was nobody around. Social scientists have long been concerned that their discipline is markedly different from natural science because the very act of observing economic and social life changes what is being observed. An anthropologist cannot observe a tribe without disturbing the rhythms of that tribe; a camera cannot watch family life without changing the dynamic of the family because its members know they are being looked at. There is even the well-known trap in economic policy that as soon as the government uses some indicator to inform policy, it becomes distorted because the markets know that indicator is being watched. All these are examples of reflexiveness – a process by which systems depart dynamically from their former balance because of the insertion of an external change agent. The very act of observation sparks an interactivity between the observer and the observed.

How is this connected with the way in which markets are conceived to work? Free market economics has its roots in a Newtonian view of the world: economic life, as Adam Smith and his disciples believed, has the same tendency to balance as the natural world. Smith argued that market prices gravitated towards 'natural' prices, which were determined by the total amount of labour spent in creating the product in question. Labour was the source of all value. In other words market prices were anchored in a natural system of values which was independent of the way prices were determined in markets, and this ensured that the market regulated itself naturally because buyers and sellers would drive the market price towards the natural price. There was an absolute standard of value which anchored the whole process. But free market economists have never established how such natural values could be reliably determined, and certainly not by reference to labour as the store of all value. So they have tried to show that the same equilibrium can be achieved not by having an ultimate source of value, but simply through a process of buyers and sellers weighing up alternatives in markets. What matters is not an absolute value, but the balance of relative values. That's enough to make markets work as Adam Smith supposed they did.

Soros's argument is that this intellectual sleight of hand does not work. If prices are not anchored in some core notion of what is cheap and what dear, then they are subject to the same reflexive forces as any other human phenomena – and the attempt to prove that markets are self-regulating is exposed as humbug. The reason why financial markets are so unstable is that price signals have a reflexive impact on the subsequent behaviour of the market. In the same way that a social scientist disturbs what he or she observes by the act of observation, so the fact of a price rising or falling becomes part of the dynamic of the market. In itself it sends a signal about valuation which changes the way the financial security is perceived; a falling share price, for example, does not necessarily send a signal that it should be bought because it is now cheaper; it also sends the signal that the market considers the underlying company is less valuable. Without perfect knowledge, the receiver of the information cannot judge if the market is right; indeed, the fall in price is more likely to send the reflexive message that the company in question is being downgraded in value and it would be as wise to endorse the judgement and sell as it would be to take the contrary view and buy. Without some independent 'natural' value, which of course is non'existent, in this reflexive universe the self-regulating properties of the market are very weak. Financial markets, as a result, overshoot upwards and downwards.

And if reflexivity is a core element in Soros's thinking, it also looms large in leading sociologist Anthony Giddens's interpretation of why contemporary life is so analytically distinct from the periods before it.[5] A 'natural' order in economics has been seen to need prices that are anchored in 'natural' values; in the same way a 'natural' order in society must necessarily be anchored in 'natural' instincts and impulses. In the eighteenth and early part of the nineteenth century both assumptions about the nature of markets and society could be plausibly made by economic and social theorists – hence Adam Smith and his view of markets, and the conservative Edmund Burke praising the enduring stability of society's small platoons. But in the last decades of the twentieth century, argues Giddens, just as markets are shot through with destabilising reflexivities and spillover effects (like the bus industry with which we began the chapter) so the same is true of society.

Society now is not rooted in any 'natural' pattern of social behaviour: what we eat is no longer determined by the seasons; gender no longer prescribes a predetermined role in families and careers; birth no longer ascribes status. As a result there are no settled patterns of behaviour; rather there are choices about courses of conduct which launch destabilising and continued dynamics both for the individual and the wider society.

Thus the changing position of women in the labour market and towards motherhood has set in train a dynamic about family structure, patterns of child-rearing and even sexual morality which cannot be contained by an insistence that we re-invent the past. We cannot stop the process by appealing to women to stay at home or to abstain from becoming single mothers. These social dynamics are in permanent process and, like the financial markets restlessly overshooting upwards and downwards, they cannot be regulated by an insistence that we return to some settled world of stable values. The stone has been thrown into the waters; the ripples are moving outwards and changing the structure of the water and our attitudes to it. There is no going back.

For this raises another important layer of complexity. To continue with women: they do not want to return to the position they once held; rather they argue correctly that social structures should be modified to accommodate the tensions released by their change in status. If children are shown to need a 'mother' at home to help with homework and child-rearing after school, then 'mother' needs to be redefined as 'parent' – implying a sharing of the role between men and women. The reflexive dynamic of women's participation in the labour market generates another reflexive dynamic – a demand that the male role in the family change, and with it men's role in the labour market as well.

The parallel with market contracting in the economic sphere is apt. Markets should be envisioned not as means to produce successive points of balance with an inbuilt tendency to regulate themselves, but as in a constant state of reflexive experimentation with no point of balance – rather like the relationship between men and women. They are forever triggering dynamics in different spheres, prompting changes in technology, widening inequality, creating monopoly, breaking down monopoly, getting entrapped in wild enthusiasms or periods of despair, forcing change, inventing new products, demanding new responses from other competitors and so on. The creativity and adaptability of market capitalism lies in its openness to these rhythms and motions – and in permitting the responses. Capitalism has many weaknesses, but on one thing you can rely: it is always contemporary, or, as Giddens would put it, modern.

But, as Keynes and Soros emphasise, you can praise capitalism for its creativity and modernity, and even recognise that it forces new efficiencies, whilst simultaneously acknowledging that these cross-currents, trends and cascades of market events can have spill-over effects on both the economy and society which the community will at least want to shape or perhaps even avoid. Remember the example of buses and BSE with which we began the chapter. And you cannot expect two parties to any contract to solve the problem by incorporating the costs which they impose on others by freely adjusting their contract. Why should they? Even if they wanted to, how would they begin to know what the costs were that they might impose on others but that they should try to bear themselves? It is difficult enough to design a contract robust enough to take into account all the eventualities that might happen between two parties – let alone what might happen to anybody else.[6]

Here enters the other great feature of individual contracts. We don't know the future. It is unpredictable precisely because we know that 'reflexive' market capitalism itself is unpredictable. The way that men and women deal with the unpredictability of the future when they aim to live with each for long enough to rear children is typically to contract to marry; this is a statement that whatever the unpredictable circumstances of the future they will underwrite a mutual compact to stand by each other with a contractual guarantee that is recognisable in law. The relationship only works if there is trust, but the marriage contract underwrites the trust. It offers an insurance against an unknowable future, vital in the lifelong business of childrearing and parenting, but it also provides society's way of attempting to ensure that there is a structure for parenting that is undertaken by the parents, and not offloaded in a manner which is costly to society. The institution of marriage, and the nature of the contract between men and women, may now itself be 'reflexively' changing – but no one doubts that society has an interest in whatever the emerging contract may be. Your children are part of my future.

This ethic of trust is equally vital in the wider economy and wider society. As in marriage, it is the crucial element in solving the problem of constructing contracts with an unknowable future and which can set in motion dynamics that nobody wants. For example, it may be impossible to specify in a contract between a shareholder and a company, or between an employer and worker what the responsibilities to each other should be in the event of some shock – say a takeover approach or a recession. But both know that if they could reproduce a trust contract like marriage they would be better equipped to face an unknowable future. If a firm could trust its shareholders to refuse a takeover approach while its profits were temporarily depressed during a period of investment or restructuring, then it would be more likely to go ahead with the action. If workers knew that in a recession they could trust the firm not to lay them off (as long, say, as they offered some temporary wage cut in return), then it would be worth their while to retrain and upgrade their skills. Trust is the key ingredient to stop contract capitalism dissolving into a hire-and-fire, slash-and-burn market jungle. For the more solid a trust relationship, then the more solid the implicit contract that, whatever shocks the relationship may receive, neither party is going to desert the other. Both sides are committed.

Trust is a 'soft' idea, and economists instinctively recoil from the importance of its role. It cannot be reduced to algebraic equations, nor is it easy to build. It is part of a community's social capital, as Francis Fukuyama[7] argues, and has deep historical and cultural roots; but that does not mean that we cannot act to shape institutions and patterns of behaviour which are more likely to generate trust than others. A community with a vigorous local democracy which allows plenty of opportunity to work co-operatively to produce local results is more likely to generate trust – and experience of how trust relationships are beneficial – which spills over into economic and social affairs than one without such opportunities. This is an argument that Robert Putnam has made forcibly about the impact of the introduction of strong regional government in Italy.[8] And as I shall argue in Chapter 3, ways are open to the British to think creatively about how to stimulate more trust – both in the design of our firms and our democracy.

But there is another element in this conception of markets that is rather 'harder' – namely the key role of market structure and firms' strategies in determining the pattern of competition and how reflexive dynamics are shaped. Firms cannot be visualised as simple profit-maximisers in a broadly stable market; rather they are being buffeted about by all the varying violent cross-currents and eddies that this chapter has been describing, never knowing what is going to hit them next. It could be a price war, a change in the technology of production, or the entry of an unexpectedly powerful new competitor into the market. Thus an important element in the way reflexivity works itself out at the level of industries and firms is the distribution of economic power between firms. What is their market share? How able are they to cross-subsidise their operations in one market with profits from another? Once you know this, it is possible to imagine whether their best rational strategy is defensive or aggressive. We begin to enter the realms of what is known as game theory, the modelling of firm behaviour, and we also open up a new area of policy. It is imperative that competition in a market economy is distorted as little as possible by excessive monopoly power.

As for the dynamics beyond the firm that affects others, at heart the issue is about offsetting the inefficient distribution of risk. The first task is to design a system of property rights in which obligations to the wider community are built into the core idea of property, so that, for example, firms are obliged to take into account the interests of wider stakeholders in their decisions. The second task is to build collective insurance systems to underwrite collective risk, with the definition of insurance cast as widely as possible to include education, health and housing along with unemployment insurance. The better designed and well funded the systems of collective insurance, then the more the degree of unfair risk faced by those on average and below average incomes is ameliorated.

In short the trick in constructing a successful capitalism is to harness flexibility and commitment, even though the two values are in tension. And because capitalism is a dynamic system which has an innate capacity to run away with itself in reflexive patterns of behaviour, to institute countervailing dynamics that offset those trends. Before we examine in detail what those policies and instruments might be, we need to look more closely at how contemporary capitalism is working – and just how extensive and destructive are the reflexive patterns of contract capitalism launched by the new right over the last eighteen years.

The System in Action: The Labour Market

Perhaps the least-well-understood impact of reflexive contract capitalism is the way it generates inequality, and that this growing inequality is itself a source of economic inefficiency. Typically Conservatives resist both claims, arguing that inequality is a necessary attribute of any successful capitalism because it needs strong rewards for success and penalties for failure, and that the costs are vastly overstated because while the gap between the top and bottom 10 per cent may be widening, the same people do not stay at the bottom over time. Critics of growing inequality, they allege, fail to understand its dynamic nature.

In fact we understand it too well. There are two reflexive processes at work, one at the bottom and the other at the top, which far from promoting social mobility lead to a trap at the bottom and an increasingly closed élite at the top. In economic terms talent is becoming seriously misallocated as unreasonably high rewards at the top in some favoured sectors attract too many of the skilled and qualified to crowd into them, while those at the bottom churn from unemployment and inactivity to semi-employment and back again – representing a de-skilled underclass which cannot fully participate in the economy and society. And while those at the bottom develop their own sub-culture, in which petty crime and drug-taking are increasingly legitimate, those at the top have developed a culture of opting out in which their increasing caste status causes them to withdraw from the public life of the country. An educational, health and housing system grows around their needs, feeding their élite position. Inequality becomes a cancer, gnawing away at the economic and social vitality of the nation.

At the top are emerging what Professors Robert Frank and Philip Cook call winner-takes-all markets.[9] Top performers in professions as disparate as the law and football, hospital surgery and investment banking are earning even higher salaries in relation to the average. More and more high-quality people are flocking to these sectors, however poor their prospects of reaching the summit, because the indifferent odds are more than compensated for by the exceptional rewards. Meanwhile there is a parallel fall-away in the quality of recruits in engineering, the Civil Service and teaching. But the economic returns to the wider society from these areas are as great as, or greater, than those with winner-takes-all markets. Frank and Cook estimate, for example, that a doubling of student numbers in engineering would increase US gross domestic product by 0·5 per cent, while a doubling in those of law students would cause it to decline by 0·3 per cent. Inequality is leading to a serious economic malfunction.

Here again we see the malign impact of an over-reliance on the contract model to generate efficiency, and what happens when individualism is accentuated and the trust ethic becomes degraded. It has always been true that there are some industries and activities where the value of a superstar can have a dramatic impact on the performance of the organisation – a proven goal scorer, a winner of merger and acquisition business, a surgeon who pulls off remarkable operations, and so on. What is different today is that the stars can insist on individual contracts, in which they get a larger share of the profits they contribute to the organisation; rather than be part of an overall pay structure, in the contract culture they can negotiate their own rewards. In an individualist society there is less shame in denying the role of others in your success and insisting upon the unalloyed importance of your own efforts. Moreover, with rapid communications it is more transparent who the deal-maker or play-maker is – and other organisations are less shameless about coming forward to poach potential winners, strengthening the winners' bargaining power.

And of course the winner-takes-all dynamic applies to the organisation too; if a firm can get into a virtuous circle in which success generates success the pay-offs are very much higher than they used to be, hence the importance of possessing the star performers. Today's communications relay the news of success much faster, opening up more immediate opportunities to exploit it, so that any virtuous circle works much more quickly than before, with more explosive results. The effect is spreading to sectors which hitherto have been protected. For example, British universities are now keen to attract top research professors to their staffs in order to improve their research ratings and allocations of funds; the introduction of competitive contracting for research money means more competitive contracting for research superstars – and so the salaries of the chosen few are driven remarkably high, at least in comparison to other academics if not stock-market traders!

Although the winners are plainly better off in this new universe, the knock-on consequences are malign. Startling disparities in income undermine the cohesiveness of organisations, and attack the basic conception of the work ethic because winner-takes-all salaries are so wildly disproportionate to the efforts made by those who earn them – as evident now in universities as in investment banks. The Bank of England, for example, has recently deplored the excessive salaries paid to leading traders in the financial markets; the trend gives them the incentive to take risks that will boost their salaries if they succeed but hurt the firm if they lose – and the emergence of teams of traders, fund managers and analysts moving from bank to bank in search of ever wilder salaries and bonuses is inflating the cost base of the City. In the long run the process will undermine the competitiveness of the entire financial services industry.

The winner-takes-all culture intrudes into the quick of the broader culture, as film studios, publishers and television all compete for proven winners rather than innovate. They understand the importance of getting inside the virtuous circle and look for quick market success; new authors, scripts and series which might need perseverance, but which would enrich our culture, are neglected, while those with a successful track record are focused on. In the wider society, as the message spreads that the rewards of élite status are so high, the battle for élite qualifications to step on the first rung of the ladder becomes more intense. Middle-class parents become chronically neurotic and increasingly aggressive about their children's educational progress, knowing that they must win in the scramble to attend élite universities and private schools in order to give their children the chance of becoming winners. Here is a classic case in which reflexive economic behaviour starts a chain that ends up intruding into parent-child relationships; all because top people's pay has become as subject to contract, individualism and lack of trust as the rest of our new contract capitalism.

But if this is happening at the top, there is a comparable development at the bottom, which is driven by the same forces. As argued earlier, one of the claims of Conservative apologists is that even if it is true that the poorest 10 per cent are 13 per cent worse off in real terms now than they were in 1979, then that doesn't matter because the same people are not in the bottom 10 per cent. They may start poor, but the best fight to get out of that situation.

The claim is unfounded, for it neglects how little above the bottom 10 per cent the supposedly upwardly mobile manage to rise, and the very short period of time that they manage to stay there. There is certainly churning at the bottom as the very poor find some form of work, but the chances of moving up the income scale or of not going back into poverty are extremely low. As Sarah Jarvis and Stephen Jenkins of the ESRC Research Centre of Micro-social Change at the University of Essex have proved,[10] the movement up and down the income scale – whoever you are – does not go very far. It is true that in any one year half the bottom 20 per cent move up the income scale – but in the next year 30 per cent move back down again, and more the year afterwards. Jarvis and Jenkins calculated that over a third of British adults had dipped into the bottom fifth of income earners for one year during the four-year period between 1991 and 1994, and then circulated back out again. But a bedrock of around 7 per cent of the population is permanently stuck at the bottom, of whom a quarter are single parents and 30 per cent are couples with children. Richard Dickens of the LSE goes further: he shows that wage mobility has *fallen* since the mid-1970s.

The picture is of a large number of people circulating between unemployment and semi-employment and then back into unemployment, and not getting paid well either. Almost none of the jobs the unemployed obtain is full-time and very few carry hourly wage rates above £4 an hour. According to the *Employment Audit*, published by the think tank at the Employment Policy Institute, over half those claiming unemployment benefit have claimed benefit in the previous twelve months.[11]

What propels this *demi-monde* of churning poor is labour market contracting, which has recently been accentuated by the new job seekers' allowance – an overt contract in which the unemployed promise to search for and accept any available job in return for unemployment payments which they receive as a matter of right for only six months. In other words, a collective system of insurance has been corroded into a contract in which the recipient accepts the individual responsibility to look for work in return for income, the assumption being that there is always work if you look hard enough. But it is a very one-sided bargain; there is no symmetrical obligation on the state to offer training or to stimulate a flow of reasonably paid jobs.

Thus the contracting recipient of income support goes into a labour market where protection and regulation are weak, to pick up low-paid, unskilled contract work. This is commoditisation of labour at its worst – the bundling up of work into units of low-paid labour time where the risk of adjusting the labour force to changes in demand is borne wholly by the employee. There is no incentive to train or upgrade skills because the pay-offs are so low.

Here, as at the top, there is an exponential reflexiveness, but it is driving wages down in a race to the bottom. Industries like retailing, distribution, catering and hotels find they can offer price advantages and win market share by lowering their wage costs; and, given that there is a large pool of weak and defenceless labour compelled to accept any wage under the new job seekers' allowance, and with the wages councils abolished, they bid down hourly wage rates. It is a symbiotic relationship: the industries need the labour, but because of the imbalance of power between the contracting parties, the employees help to create the industries that rely on them.

Nor is that all. The Audit Commission's recent report[12] revealed that a third of children now live in families below the poverty line. It is a hand-to-mouth existence, with a poor diet, inadequate clothing and indifferent housing. The chances of children moving out of the section of the population into which they were born are negligible. State schools are weakening while élite schools strengthen. These children are more or less condemned to repeat the same cycle of churning in and out of semi-employment and family break-up in the next generation.

Nor does this emerging inequality need to be explained by reference to competition from low-wage countries, technological innovation or changes to the tax and benefit system. All these add to the brew, certainly, but the heart of the process is generated by the new contracting labour market structures and their interaction, as we will see, with the impulses from the capital markets. Nor is income inequality alone affected, there is also growing job insecurity and the wider sense that the world of work is riskier.

This is now highly controversial territory, with one side – ranging from a curious alliance of the European Commission, the Conservative party, liberal and conservative economists, and the Labour MP Frank Field – claiming that not much has changed (even while the Conservative party hymns the new flexible labour market), and the other side insisting that there has been a substantial change to the number of jobs people hold over their careers and thus their tenure in any given job.

At first sight the figures support the no-changers, whose argument has been plausibly assembled by the *Sunday Times* Conservative loyalist, economics editor David Smith.[13]

From 1975 to 1995 the average length of time a job was held fell from 6 years 1 month to just 5 years 6 months, hardly an earth-shattering confirmation that work is more insecure and one which, with a range of similar figures, allows Smith to argue that insecurity is a will-o'-the-wisp. But look more closely and a different pattern emerges. Men aged over 50, for example, used to hold a job for 18 years 3 months in 1975; in 1995 that had collapsed to 12 years 10 months. Indeed all men have experienced a fall in the period they can expect to hold a job; while women, except those aged under 24, have all seen an improvement, so that the experience of the sexes is converging and keeping the average high. Put another way, while women can expect to hold 11 jobs over their working lives, men can now expect to hold 10 – when 20 years ago the average was 7.[14]

And while it may not seem much that job tenure has fallen from 8 to 6 years on average for men over the last 20 years, think of the analogy of the bath. To cool a hot bath you have to run nothing but cold water for a long time; to produce such a fall in average male job tenure every new job has to be in one form or another insecure. The labour market for those who enter it and those who are compelled to move jobs in it is changing very rapidly; and men's experience, as the traditional breadwinners historically holding more full-time jobs, is a more accurate reflection of the underlying trends than the swelling numbers of women working, who while closing the gap with men, are still treated unequally.

Full-time tenured employment is under assault, an experience which can be confirmed in any bar or office in the country. Not only that, but the proportion of men with tenures of under 2 years has risen by 12 per cent. The churning cited earlier is also picked up in the figures: 8 per cent of workers left jobs within 3 months in 1975, but now the number has nearly doubled, ranging from a low of 14 per cent to a high of 22 per cent in the period from 1984 to 1993.

There is more insecurity.[15]

Nor is that surprising. The lack of labour market protection, the weakness of unions and the intense pressure on private- and public-sector companies alike to improve their profitability and efficiency have meant that the fashionable doctrine of downsizing has spread like a contagion. Companies are designing their employment contracts so that they have as few full-time staff members as possible, and offer contracts to other workers which emphasise that the contracts can be broken or rewritten if trading conditions change. And as soon as one company behaves in this way, especially if it is the market leader, there is a ripple effect across the industry, with everybody having to benchmark their costs besides that example. Whatever a manager's own personal view of the matter, competition compels him or her to follow suit, or else that particular enterprise's costs get out of line and bankruptcy results.

In *The State We're In* I developed the idea of a 30/30/40 society with 30 per cent of adults either unemployed or economically inactive, 30 per cent in jobs where one way or another tenure is insecure – and only 40 per cent who have tenure, ranging from self-employment to full-time employment, which could be regarded as reasonably secure. The groupings have proved robust with the *Employment Audit* recently validating the categorisation, although some critics[16] say that much less has changed over the past twenty years than I argue; that the most rapid expansion of part-time work was in the 1970s and the decline in full-time tenured work was most marked in the 1980s. However, both points neglect the dramatic change in the role of men in the labour market: one in four adult men are now unemployed or economically inactive, with the result that men are nearly as numerous in the bottom 30 per cent as women – a transformation of their position.

As for the middle 30 per cent of newly insecure, it is the unfair distribution of risk that is the issue. It is not merely the probability of involuntarily losing a job that matters, it is the consequences. As income inequality has risen to ever greater heights so the penalty in terms of loss of income on job changes has risen; the Employment Policy Institute's *Employment Audit* estimates that on average any new job after severance generally carries earnings some 20 per cent below the old level, and that fewer than three in ten new jobs are permanent and full-time. And those who find new work have been unemployed for 20 per cent longer than in the 1970s.

Nor do the penalties stop there. Employers, themselves under intense competitive pressure, try to avoid offering the generous perks that were characteristic of the 1960s and 1970s. Full-time employment rights are not what they were. Holiday, pension and sickness benefits are being pared back, forcing workers to rely on the protection of the welfare state or to supplement it with their own insurance policies.

Here too the environment has become riskier. Unless you live on Mars it is quite clear that the welfare state is less comprehensive than it was. Social-security payments are continually falling behind the growth of real wages, indexed only to prices. In short the penalties for being sick or out of work are higher than they used to be.

And here is a further problem which the defenders of the *status quo* don't mention. As job tenures shorten, so there are growing periods in most careers with either little or no income; it becomes harder to maintain the very expensive insurance payments that individuals have to assume if they want to make good the shortages of the welfare state. Indeed these are so expensive that they are beyond the reach of most people. In sum the penalties for losing a job are higher. The public safety net is weaker and any private substitute is very expensive and the coverage poor. Men in particular are having a much tougher time. There is more risk; there is more inequality; and it matters.

The System in Action: The Financial Markets

Rising inequality does not just impose costs on the economy through over-rewarding the rich, trapping the poor in poverty, provoking the undervaluation of acquiring skills and infecting the economy, society and culture with a heightened sense of unfair risk – it also unbalances the rhythm of economic activity. Inequality in Britain distributes income unfairly not only between classes but between regions, with London and the Home Counties markedly richer than the rest of the country. They rapidly overheat before the rest of the United Kingdom in the upturn phase of the economic cycle and cool off sharply in the downturn. The issue for policy-makers is always whether to act to depress the south-eastern economy before the rest of the United Kingdom moves into the upturn, or to stimulate it when the rest of the country is depressed. If the pattern of economic activity across the country were more even, then the economy could be more successfully managed.

The problem is that the British economy is weak. Britain invests less than its major competitors and tends to favour low-risk investment in real estate and trading to high-risk innovation at the frontier of technology. With a weak capacity to lift production, the economy quickly runs into bottlenecks in economic upturns, with one sector or region overheating before the rest. But the rate and character of investment in the real economy is closely related to the contract-based financial system, which is almost wholly organised around a system of highly 'liquid' markets, providing investors in other words with the chance to recoup any commitment they have made quickly and turn it into cash by selling. The financial markets undervalue future profits and encourage the takeover of a very high proportion of UK companies, while British banks tend to lend short term. The cumulative impact on the real economy is marked. Contract capitalism is proving as destructive here as in the labour market.

However, defenders of the system argue that the rate of business investment in Britain is only fractionally lower than in our competitors and that the problem is not high financial returns but rather low levels of profitability. If there is short-termism it is generated as much by management as by the financial markets and that pension funds and insurance companies do not buy and sell shares very frequently. They go on to argue that takeover is an effective way of ensuring that assets are used well; that companies get all the bank finance they need; and if they wanted more long-term loans the system would readily provide them. At least part of the problem, they insist, is that Britain has a volatile economy, making investors very cautious about stumping up cash for projects which may become unprofitable because of a fall in demand outside the company's control. And anyway, whatever the merits that financial systems like Japan's and Germany's once had, those days are over. Globalisation is prompting a convergence of financial systems to the Anglo-Saxon norm.

The arguments are instantly recognisable as falling into one of three ideological categories in Conservative thought. The first cluster falls under the rubric of efficiency: takeover, short-term bank finance and all the rest are defended as spurs to a narrow accountant's view of efficiency, and spill-over effects are ignored because they are not part of the Conservative system. The second cluster is grouped under the notion that markets solve problems and are only prevented from doing so by external factors, so that it is managers who cause short-termism, the economy which has been managed badly by politicians and is too volatile, and labour market regulations and trade unions which have depressed profits. If they didn't exist, the system would work much better. The third category is the denial-of-facts school (because they fall outside the politically correct worldview of the right) – investment really is not lower in Britain than elsewhere and the German and Japanese financial systems are remodelling themselves on Britain. This is fanciful indeed.

The case needs to be restated – and the next few pages are devoted to this task. In 1992, the last year for which comparable figures are available, the capital stock per head in Germany was $50,116, in Japan $41,286 and in the United States $35,993. In Britain it stood at $22,509.[17] The value added per worker in Germany was £30,200, in Japan £31,212 and in Britain £17,756.[18] British Research and Development expenditure is some 2.2 per cent of gross domestic product – below France, Germany, Japan and the United States.[19] The government claims that private-sector business investment, expressed as a proportion of GDP, is close to the average of the major industrial powers; but British figures are inflated because of the inclusion of whole sectors which have been privatised but which in other countries remain in the public sector. Even if the claim was true, which it is not, investment would still not be high enough. If Britain is to catch up, it has to raise the volume and character of its investment *above* those of its competitors over decades, even while it makes its existing stock more efficient. The figures don't lie.

My contention is that, given the current structure of the financial system, the prospects of this taking place are slim, verging on nil. The argument is not that pension funds and insurance companies are intrinsically short-termist and greedy, bleeding British companies dry by their demand for high dividends, or that banks are venal and overcautious institutions which cannot prevent themselves from undermining their customers. Rather it is that there is a complex interaction between the pattern of share ownership, the structure of taxation, the liquidity of the markets and the framework of company law in which every individual actor can behave rationally and even decently, but which still produces the perverse outcome of less investment and output growth than the optimum.

As argued earlier, trust is a key ingredient in the successful firm; strong trust relationships help workers, suppliers and financiers to commit themselves to the firm and to resist unexpected shocks. In return this enables the firm to be more secure in making long-run investment decisions, which are necessarily hazardous, and make it happier to run lower margins on the goods and services it sells. The higher the trust, the more likely the firm is to have high investment and growth in sales. The pole around which trust turns is the commitment of the owner. If there is one owner, or a family owner, then the commitment is self-evident; it is likely that the investment will represent a considerable part of the owner's fortune, that the relationship will be personal and the owner will care about his or her reputation. If the company is sold, it will be well trailed in advance so the stakeholders in the enterprise will be able to plan for it. And if the owner does not use the resources in the firm well, then it will lose ground in the marketplace. You do not need competition for ownership as well as competition for the firm's goods, the latter is quite enough to secure competitiveness.

The same is true if there are hundreds of thousands of small shareholders as owners. Anyone can sell without the sale endangering the future of the company; the broad base of share ownership allows the same continuity of control and management, and if a takeover approach comes it is harder for the predator to persuade perhaps hundreds of thousands of shareholders of the merits of their case.

The shareholder and trust relationship pattern is unstable when ownership falls between these two extremes, which is the British case, and as is persuasively argued by Colin Mayer[18], is the root of the British problem. Extraordinarily, some 70 per cent of company equity is owned by financial institutions like pension funds, insurance companies and unit trusts. Some management is delegated to investment management companies, but the larger pension funds and insurance companies perform their own management in-house. As a result ownership responsibilities are discharged, for most companies, by no more than thirty or forty decision-makers.

These are large shareholdings, certainly, but they fall a long way short of having the same influence and commitment as a sole proprietor; on the other hand they are far too large for any one of their buying and selling decisions not to have an impact on the company. For example, it makes takeover much easier because there are typically fewer than thirty investment management companies whose approval have to be sought for a majority of supportive votes to be won. But equally the number of shareholders is unstably high if the company tries to avoid takeover by persuading a sub-group of shareholders to stand by the company when it is in difficulty. For example if the sub-group is prepared to support the company through the period of depressed profits, dividends and share price while the necessary change of direction is executed, they risk some of the other shareholders outside the sub-group piggy-backing off their efforts. They can sell and then buy back at a lower price while the committed shareholders ride out the storm, sustaining losses that the defecting shareholders do not experience. They boost their relative investment performance and win more business as a result. British institutional shareholders, through no fault of their own, have power without responsibility.

The difficulty is that this ownership structure intersects with the highly liquid, contract-based stock market. It is phenomenally easy to buy and sell large volumes of shares; and everyone knows it. A pension fund may have supported a company for twenty years, but it can sell its entire holding in a matter of minutes; and, as described above, even if the pension-fund managers want to be committed, far-sighted owners they risk the possibility that others do not. They face the penalty that their investment funds will not perform as well as their competitors if they do not follow the same ruthless logic and sell if the price is right.

These tendencies would be softened if British company law offered other means for shareholders to express their long-term relationship with the company, for example through being required to elect their own representatives to the board as non-executive directors. But no such legal requirement exists, and in any case most British companies would prefer an arms' length relationship with their shareholders rather than have them on the board as watchful guardians of their interests. This might make them more committed to the company, but it also might lead to challenges and disagreements that directors would rather avoid in the name of board cohesiveness – even if the greater prize is greater shareholder commitment.

Nor does the taxation structure help. Pension funds are exempt from tax; indeed, the curious British treatment of the taxation of dividends means that they benefit from high distribution of dividends, being able to claim back tax that would otherwise have gone to the government. They pay no capital gains tax on the disposal of their assets either. In short, as tax-exempt zones they have every incentive to look for immediate gains and none to behave in a committed long-term manner.

The interaction of these incentives and institutional biases reinforces a process that persistently favours the near-term, the deal with quick returns and the takeover. This is not to argue that every British company is run in this way, or that investment is non-existent; but it is to describe the bias in the system to financial values over those of production and innovation, so that at the margin a dividend pay-out is preferred to an additional pound of research and development, an extra profit now is preferred to higher profits in the future. This is why British companies tend to look for higher returns over shorter periods than their international competitors and why, under intense pressure to minimise their costs, they are under such constant pressure to downsize and reduce their core labour force. Even if they are not under direct threat of takeover themselves, they have to run the business so that there is as little extra profit to be squeezed from the company as possible: they are compelled to manage as shadow predators to avoid the real thing.

It is not sufficient, as the Conservative party argues supported by the like of Professor Tim Congdon, to claim that the existing stock of investment is being used ever more efficiently even if it is small, and that this is the result of pressure from the financial markets, so therefore the financial markets are 'good'.[21] Far from liquidity having any malign affect on investment, he says, there is a correlation between the degree to which an economy is under-developed and the under-development of the stock market. Stock markets encourage investment, because they offer investors the chance to reverse their decision to buy shares and turn the purchase back into cash every minute of every trading day. Nor does he accept that the stock market and the threat of takeover forces companies to make high returns; if anything, he says, returns in Britain are low rather than high.

But Tim Congdon misunderstands my argument. The issue is not whether liquidity is a 'good thing'; it is vital in reassuring investors that they can reverse a lending or investment decision if they choose – and so enables them to bring forward investment in financial assets. The point, as argued above, is rather how liquidity interacts with the pattern of company ownership, company law and owners' incentives.

That is what produces short termism, not liquidity by itself.

Congdon goes on to object that if British business did seek such high returns, then the return on capital would be higher than the derisory 10 per cent or so registered in Britain[22] – but this is seriously to misread the chain of causation. Financial returns are closely related to the overall level of demand and the financial structure of the underlying enterprise, as every mortgage borrower knows. Just as it pays to have a high mortgage in a rising property market to get the best returns, so heavily borrowed business sectors will always make higher returns than lightly borrowed business sectors for any given rise in demand. British companies are underborrowed, operating in a country where output and investment tend to be low.

Their low returns on capital are at the end of a process which has been initiated, in part, by the very demanding financial criteria that are set for new investment and the short termism of British bank loans. Britain has an underborrowed business sector which does not invest much because of the high returns that are required, thus creating a relatively low growth economy; the result is that less investment is undertaken, the economy grows indifferently and rates of financial return on capital are poor. This in turn makes it difficult to manage the economy with a stimulatory bias, lowering interest rates and raising government borrowing because we are continually running into bottlenecks. Congdon's view of efficiency prevents him from understanding the dynamics and spill-overs that propel modern capitalism, and the weaknesses that are created by Britain's system of finance.

Some Evidence – from North Sea Oil to Building Societies

Corporate strategies – investing overseas, seeking protected markets at home, growing by takeover, questing for monopoly – are driven by the need to satisfy the standards for high immediate financial returns. This is the axis on which the British business sector turns and it permeates everything.

For example, North Sea oil is in some respects a remarkable story. Oil has been pumped out of fields in some of the most inhospitable seas in the world. It is a triumph of engineering and technology, but the sadness is that so little of it is British. In Aberdeen, the centre of the industry, almost all the chief companies are foreign owned, with the British in the role of service providers, or the painters and decorators as they say locally. Over the last twenty years there has been a major opportunity to build up an offshore oil-supply industry, developing techniques in the construction of oil rigs, the laying of underwater pipes and even underwater robots. However, there is virtually no British representation whatsoever; our small companies have not been backed with venture-capital finance and long-term bank loans, and our large companies have been taken over. Some invested in the North Sea as little more than a tax dodge. When the industry moves to the next offshore oil-producing area, as it will when the oil runs out, no indigenous British companies will be there.

The contrast with the Norwegians could hardly be starker. A deliberate effort was made to construct an indigenous Norwegian oil industry from the Norwegian fields. The Norwegian company Kvaerner, for example, which now owns shipyards on the Clyde, took over the construction group Trafalgar House for more than £900 million in March 1996 and has a large British workforce, was a tiny company twenty-five years ago. But as its managing director Eric Tonseth told me in the Channel 4 series *False Economy*, it is the long-term committed shareholders, patient in waiting for dividends, who have been a major factor in its growth. It's important, he says, 'to have long-term shareholders who can associate with your industrial strategy'. He has been able to build up investment in research and development on a scale his British competitors could not rival, and Kvaerner has ended up the predator on the London stock exchange with British companies, which originally were larger than Kvaerner, his victims.

And if Britain's financial and ownership structures have been decisive in shaping the destiny of North Sea oil, they have also been fundamental, at the other end of the scale, in the evolution of the bus industry as we saw at the beginning of this chapter. The stock market has proved crucial for the growth of the three companies – Stagecoach, Cowie and First Bus – which now dominate more than 50 per cent of all routes in Britain. The financial system has been the handmaiden of monopolisation.

And so it goes on. The great mutual building societies and insurance companies are substituting hundreds of years of accrued capital that had the potential to be put to the benefit of the mutual members for share quotations. The share issue pays for a one-off bribe to the members to agree to demutualisation, and then the new company can enter the race to be the predator or victim in the game of takeover. Lending margins may be higher to service dividend payments, but the quote offers the chance to become part of a gigantic financial empire – or to create one. The great regional building societies are being concentrated in London, so transforming another industry. The attractive, unexpected bonuses reward individual small borrowers and savers in the short term for giving up their membership rights, but in the long run enormous centralised financial service groups, anxious to maintain dividend growth, will end up neglecting this very constituency in their customer base. Already the National Consumer Council reports that banks and building societies are withdrawing outlets from unprofitable parts of towns and cities and offering poor interest rates to small savers.[23] The quest is for high-worth customers who are good risks; low-income customers are expensive to service and their interests are neglected. Interest rates on small savings in the Co-op are significantly higher than those in mainstream quoted building societies.

The way in which the newly privatised utilities boosted profits by rounds of redundancies, and then bought back their own shares with the resulting profits and cash in a vain attempt to support the share price and stave off takeover was a classic example of the financial markets' priorities. Here the process of risk displacement was most clearly in view, with the utilities being natural monopolies which simply increased their profitability by reducing their labour force. Most of the regional electricity companies at the time of privatisation have ended up being bought willy-nilly by other utilities from both at home and abroad, and the dream of a competitive electricity supply structure has been allowed to die. It's the same story in television, supermarkets and pharmaceuticals. Contract capitalism British style promotes efficiencies, certainly, but at what cost? And to whose ultimate advantage?

The Public Sector and the Welfare State

If the labour and financial markets interact as the engines of under-investment and social marginalisation, the welfare state and public institutions offer some of the most powerful instruments to offset the process. But here the story parallels that in the private sector. The imposition of a narrow conception of efficiency has led to the contracting model being spread across the public sector, with the internal market in the National Health Service through to universal compulsory competitive tendering in local authorities, leading to some vicious inequalities. And all this has taken place in an atmosphere of overall public expenditure constraint in which the rise in social-security spending, perversely driven by the poverty 'marketisation' has created, has persistently crowded out the real growth of other programmes.

The Conservative doctrine has been that the collective insurance represented by social security is necessarily less efficient than private contracts between individuals and private insurance companies. Every effort has been made to encourage the growth of personal, private insurance and the decline in collective insurance, culminating in the Conservatives' pre-electoral proposal to privatise the state pension. The incentives to take out personal pensions represent one thrust in this policy; tax relief for some private health insurance another; the tax exemptions for private schools are a third – while systematically holding back the growth of public expenditure in these areas has made public services progressively less attractive in comparison with what is available in the private sector, and has thus encouraged workers to contract out and make individual provision.

The over-riding aim has been to reduce public expenditure as a proportion of gross domestic product, with the government pledged to lower it to below 40 per cent of GDP and some commentators pushing for a target of 30 per cent.[24] This is deemed to achieve a number of simultaneous objectives: it will promote efficiency because the roll-back of government will see an offsetting rise in market contracting; it will promote individual responsibility, which is seen as a moral good; and it will offer the prospect of lowering taxation and social charges, which are portrayed as a means of incentivising effort and a source of competitive advantage. It is a sign of the dominance of Conservative thinking that Tony Blair has taken to reminding his left-of-centre audiences that public expenditure under Attlee represented around 30 per cent of GDP, signalling that he too regards the lowering of public expenditure as a desirable target.

In the light of the evidence presented earlier this chapter, such thinking has to be regarded with extreme scepticism. It is not true *a priori* that market contracting is better than collective provision, if risks are best shared collectively. The fact that expenditure has been moved off the public balance sheet does not mean that the expenditure does not need to be made; it means merely that the burden has been displaced on to individuals, who may be in no position to assume the burden. Progressive taxes and social insurance, organised by the state, are the best means to fund pensions, education and health care, for example. Moreover, these are public goods in the best sense; important reflexive dynamics flow from them being provided by the state, in that there is some guarantee of minimum health standards, educational attainment and income in old age, sickness or unemployment. These allow individuals to accept these increasing risks associated with contemporary contract capitalism; without them the distribution of risk becomes unacceptably unfair.

Social-security spending represents some 13 per cent of GDP; education and health spending around 12 per cent. Social-security expenditure is the result of social insurance; the provision for old age and unemployment would have to be made willy-nilly; better it be made efficiently through the state. The same rule applies for both education and health expenditure, which are both arguably too low. With debt interest and defence spending, these components of government expenditure already exceed 30 per cent of GDP.

Thus, once we add the other programmes – agricultural support, public transport, overseas aid – to name just a few, the aggregate total rises towards 40 per cent of GDP. To lower public expenditure to 30 per cent therefore requires major surgery. It could not be undertaken without abandoning the principle of collective insurance in one of the key programmes of the state. This is not to mount an 'unreconstructed' defence of public expenditure; it is to argue that public spending prosecutes an important moral and social purpose and is fundamental to tackling the new and powerful dynamics of risk in contemporary capitalism.

This also has implications for taxation. In the Conservative lexicon taxation is seen as a burden to be minimised, and one which distorts 'natural' patterns of behaviour and responsibility; in truth it is a necessary mechanism in order to ensure that an equitable burden of risk is shared between the winners and losers. This does not mean that very high marginal rates of tax are tolerable; but it does mean that the next government, of whatever hue, will find it impossible to reduce taxation significantly below current levels – and will probably have to raise taxation to support current levels of spending. This is not a moral disaster. It is the down payment that we make to ensure that our society can hold together – and that the government has the ammunition to contain the powerful reflexivities which are spilling over into every corner of our lives. So what to do? It is to that question we now turn.

3
THE STATE TO COME

THE MOST INSIDIOUS doctrine of our age is that we have no choices. We are predestined to continue as we are. The only efficiency we can consider is the allocative efficiency of the market. We regulate private enterprise at our peril. We can spend public money to support education, transport, welfare and health only with reluctance; to do so threatens higher taxes, and causes sloth and inflation. We must accept unemployment, idleness and poverty stoically. The best we can do is to help individuals to help themselves. Nothing can be done that might burden 'enterprise' – whether it is asking that they train their workforce better or respect the environment more. If any such burdens are imposed, it is with the deepest foreboding and shrillest of warnings about the consequences for jobs. And as for public ownership or any form of public initiative, the idea is dead at birth. It is held to be axiomatic that private is more efficient, and a government which disputed such beliefs would be distrusted as trying to protect yesterday rather than promote tomorrow.

We live, after all, in a global market – don't we? Globalisation is the new buzzword, casting gloom or delight depending upon your perspective. For a John Redwood or the Japanese management consultant Kenichi Ohmae, who has become a one-man industry singing the praises of a 'borderless world', we live in an era in which a global market guarantees a new and fecund competition along with boundless individual opportunity. Those who believe in the desirability of government are as pessimistic as the globalisers are optimistic; the new era means the gains of the twentieth century – from the forty-hour week to a public library service – are all under threat. No country dares insist that big companies respect its regulations for fear they will migrate elsewhere; nor, for the same reason, can we levy taxes to support our public institutions. John Redwood manages to believe in both globalisation and national sovereignty simultaneously – but squares the circle because the over-riding economic action he deems necessary for a nation state is to enlarge the capacity of markets and reduce public spending. This is a peculiar definition of sovereignty – a power that can only be used in one way.

Yet there is an emerging counter-view that the globalisers have greatly overstated their case, as forthcoming books and articles by John Gray, David Held and his Open University colleagues, and the Nexus group will all emphasise.[1] There are choices still to be made, even while we can see that the world is changing rapidly. It may be true, as some sceptics about globalisation argue, that the world economy has always been international, but what we are witnessing today is something more than an acceleration of long-established trends. Whether in trade, finance or the speed and scope of communication, the degree of interpenetration of national markets and cultures is unprecedented. We smoke Marlboro cigarettes, eat sushi, use Windows 95, experiment with acupuncture, read *Cosmopolitan*, take away pizza and watch CNN wherever we are. English is emerging as the international language of communication whether it is for air-traffic control or scientific papers; the culture of the ski-resort, dealing room and airport is homogeneous. Blue jeans, sweatshirts and trainers are ubiquitous.

Exports and imports are rising as a proportion of gross national product in every Western country, so that more and more companies rely on foreign markets for their prosperity and consumers are flattered by more choice. The volume of business in what John Gray describes as the virtual reality economy[2] – the financial derivative markets where little more than financial bets on future exchange rates, interest rates and share prices change hands – has reached trillions of dollars every year. If expectations of American interest rates change, the ripple effect cascades around the world, first in the virtual reality markets then in the real financial markets, and then in the real economy where we make our living. This is new in terms of its scale, immediacy and reach. It may be true that in the world economy before 1914 trade and finance were heavily internationalised as well, but national governments retained an economic and financial autonomy about which their contemporary counterparts can only dream.

All this is true; but there are limits to these trends, so that states and national societies still retain leverage over their destinies. *Cosmopolitan* and *Vogue*, for example, may have a universal readership, but their editors shape the basic template to meet the varying demands of different countries. Coca-Cola varies in sweetness in parts of Japan to reflect differing consumer tastes. CNN is no longer sweeping all before it as resistance grows to its highly Americanised view of the world. MTV is in decline in Asia before local demands that popular songs should be sung in local languages. Malaysia and China have both successfully insisted that Rupert Murdoch change the programming on his Asian satellite stations and broadcast in Hindi and Mandarin. Public protest in Holland, Germany and Britain forced Shell to abandon sinking the disused oil platform Brent Spa in mid-Atlantic. What is striking about key economic indicators in Western countries – from interest rates to unemployment – is how much they vary rather than how much they converge. English may be the universal language of international communication, but the more it extends its reach, the more nations wish to protect and entrench their own languages and cultures. There is increasing penetration of each other's markets and cultures, but they remain stubbornly different. Indeed, if they were not different there would be no reason for any trade.

Here the British right is guilty of an immense conceit. The presumption is that British-style capitalism is the inevitable winner in the new global market, and is the norm to which all others will inevitably converge. They will want social security systems as inexpensive as ours; trade unions as weak; company ownership systems which permit takeover to such a degree, and so on. As we have seen, a battery of tendentious figures is fired in our direction to support these claims; and if a German company chairman speaks well of investment in Britain, or another seeks a quotation on the New York stock exchange, the airwaves and newspapers are full of how German capitalism is on the point of collapse.

Yet the thrust of this book is to argue that at the very least there are substantial costs to be set against the 'efficiencies' of British capitalism, whose performance in the round is not much to celebrate, and that trying to contain the consequences is leading to an ugly degradation of our society and an assault on our liberties which Britain's unwritten constitution makes much easier. The emergence of a global market is revealing instead the variety of world capitalisms, each of which works as a system and whose component parts, apparently irrational to British eyes, make perfect sense in the context of that system. Each one has different ways of distributing the risk inherent in any form of capitalism and strikes different balances between the obligations and rights of property ownership. These particularities make sense because they are rooted in historical, political and cultural differences which persist over decades, even centuries.

To imagine that the only feasible and efficient way of organising the distribution of risk is to force individuals to insure for themselves, to run down the social security system and that efficiency demands the assertion of absolute property rights, as in Conservative Britain, is just wrong. In countries like Hong Kong or Italy the family firm is the central plank of property ownership and the family an important means of risk sharing, indeed Chinese family firms operating outside China are nearer to co-operatives than the private firms of Western Europe. In Germany ownership rights are exercised by banks and trusts, and risk shared through a powerful social security system. In the United States ownership is stock-market dominated, while risk is thrown on to the shoulders of an unskilled underclass which is systematically excluded from society. The east Asians, often praised for their cheap welfare states, rely on the family as the core provider of social insurance, while the state itself acts as a very active entrepreneur and initiator of capitalist endeavour. No capitalist country can avoid the question of how property rights are exercised or risk distributed; the two issues are at the heart of any capitalist system. Indeed one of the paradoxes of the new world order is that it allows differences in risk distribution, income inequality and 'fairness' to be sustained as much as competed away.

For example, if a country like Germany wishes to have, say, high social charges to sustain its welfare state, then it can have them – but at the price of a lower mark. The all-powerful currency markets in 1996 and 1997 have secured such a large devaluation of the mark that Germany is once again competitive, despite the hysteria about its sclerotic labour markets and loyalty to the values of the social chapter. German chemical and car firms have been careful to locate low-skill manufacture in low-cost countries while retaining skilled, labour-intensive production within Germany, so that the national comparative advantage of the German training system becomes more not less important as globalisation progresses. Germany is using the system to sustain its social market economy as much as having it competed away.

The multinational company is thus on the horns of a permanent dilemma. If it is to succeed, the company must respect local conditions which are likely to endure over time – but it will necessarily come from a very different economy and society, whose values it inevitably embodies. The genuine transnational is hard to find. Two of the most substantial surveys on multinationals both concluded that none of the companies is truly global, all are rooted in the cultures and ownership priorities of the country in which they are based; there is even some evidence that they are retrenching around their regional part of the global economy.[3] The Japanese cannot escape their commitment to manufacture and their powerful loyalty to Japan; the Americans are in thrall to the New York stock exchange and the necessity of enlarging earnings per share year by year. Wherever they operate in the world they remain in essence Japanese and American companies.

On the plus side they bring employment, investment and a desire to be a good British corporate citizen, to be as British as their local competitors. One of the aims, after all, of having a local presence is to customise products for local use and to exploit local skills; IBM, for example, has had important research facilities in Britain. On the minus side they are here to compete against local companies and to deny market share to their rivals in the global battle for supremacy. Most of the important research and development facilities remain at home, with any discoveries made in Britain exported back immediately for exploitation by the mother company. Typically, especially among Asian multinationals, British plants are used to import high-tech equipment from home-based suppliers, thereby strengthening the domestic economy. British companies investing overseas care much less about the domestic British economy; their objective is profit maximisation. Inward investment thus simultaneously strengthens and hollows out the economy in which it is directed.

Thus the balance sheet of power between the nation state and the world market is very complex. From the perspective of the multinational the new environment is as hazardous as it is seen from the viewpoint of a national government. Certainly any multinational worth its salt bargains for the best deal for any new investment in terms of subsidies and relaxed regulations by threatening to invest elsewhere, but this is a ploy of last resort. It wants to be seen as a good citizen, and threatening the nuclear option of disinvestment too frequently weakens its negotiating position. But as importantly, no company can feel safe in a global market. New technologies, markets and companies are constantly throwing up new challenges; everybody has observed how even the mighty IBM lost its dominant position within a decade and that the same forces may now be at work on McDonald's. In this climate even the biggest multinational needs allies and partners and amongst the most reliable is the nation state.

The state is therefore not just a supplicant in its relationship with multinational business. The companies may need the state as an ally to change the terms of an international trade arrangement, to turn a blind eye to a monopoly position or to give support while a new project is developed. Moreover, in a global market a better ally may be a foreign government rather than the company's own home government. The Malaysian government has been a powerful partner in constructing its new multi-media super corridor, while British high-tech companies have found the North Carolina state government a better ally in its aim to build the famous research triangle park than Britain. The British government, on the other hand, has been a more willing supporter of Rupert Murdoch than the Australian, as it has of Japanese car producers needing an advocate for their interests in the European Union.

In this terrain most analysis of globalisation is surprisingly glib, for while the nation state is clearly weaker in its capacity to run its national economy as it chooses, its capacity to initiate partnerships, regulate activity, cut deals and even fix tax rates and spending levels is still significant. Indeed there is no other player on the horizon with the same power. The British government, for example, may be fairly helpless about setting the exchange rate at a level it chooses unless it is prepared to sacrifice the achievement of other economic targets to that end, but, by allocating take-off and landing slots at Heathrow, say, it can have substantial influence over the fortunes of British Airways and other international carriers.

In sum nation states have palpably less autonomy than they did, but it would be wrong to portray them as powerless. What has changed is the risks and rewards of particular kinds of conduct, and the ways they have to be executed. Thus rewards from the old-fashioned 'Keynesian' boost to an economy through low interest rates and high government borrowing – what have been mistakenly called Keynesian economic policies even though Keynes argued that such policies were for emergencies rather than to be built permanently into the policy armoury – are much less than they used to be. For a start much more of any demand boost leaks abroad as imports come pouring in; but the capital markets also have their say. If they believe that any particular country's policy is imprudently more expansionary than other countries', and the inflation outlook is worse, then they will sell that country's currency and the financial assets they hold; the resulting financial crisis will force a reversal of policy. The risks of expansion in one country are thus much higher than they were; and the rewards comparatively paltry. Consequently any one country by itself is forced by the current complex of forces to adopt conservative government monetary and fiscal policies. In this sense globalisation has narrowed policy options.

But in other areas the decline of autonomy is exaggerated. Multinationals want to be in Britain, and know that success depends on respecting local conditions. If they leave, they surrender the market to their competitors. They may be able to supply the United Kingdom from a low-cost base in a third country, but this necessitates bearing the costs of closure in Britain and expansion abroad. Nor is it easy to reproduce the networks of trust that any enterprise builds around itself and which become part of its capacity to function well as a business. There are important advantages to a Sony or Ford of being seen as a *de facto* British company, and of designing products to meet specific British conditions embedded in local British networks. They will be lost by disinvestment, negating the whole point of the original decision to invest in Britain. BMW, for example, which now owns Rover, could not move production back to Germany or to a low-cost alternative without nullifying the purpose of buying into a British identity.

In other words, there is a spectrum of possible policy manoeuvres open to national governments which can achieve their ends even in today's environment. Indeed even while the financial markets may be intolerant of continuing high budget deficits or inflation, they tend to allow a wide spectrum of choices over tax rates and spending levels. Moreover benchmarking goes both ways. If British performance is better than the average, then economic alternatives can be enlarged – and a British government can use the examples of other countries both to inform policy and to persuade domestic interest groups of the imperative of changing. If British educational standards are lower than elsewhere, or transport is much worse – and in a global environment such comparisons are more vivid – then that requires action that might otherwise be avoided.

In some respects governments' options are greater because there is no overall binding set of rules. Everyone is making it up as they go along, and certainly no one company or one state can regard itself so powerful – not even the United States – that it has no need to compromise or reach an accommodation with others. Any company that refuses to invest in Britain because, say, it has signed the Social Chapter, risks a competitor filling the market opportunity it abjures and so losing some market share that will weaken it globally. Business cannot afford to be ideological.

Nor can it neglect the fact that it needs sound rules of the game to prosper. Even the great champions of Anglo-Saxon free-market financial capitalism do not seriously wish to privatise the IMF and World Bank, and leave the world with no multilateral government lender of last resort – a caution more than amply justified when without the IMF there could have been no $30 billion bail-out of Mexico in early 1995. Had Mexico collapsed it would have triggered a very severe banking crisis in the United States, with possible world ramifications. Nor is that all. Strong communications and transport systems, a well-educated workforce and networks of publicly funded universities and research institutes are attractions not just to domestic business but also to multinationals. They too benefit from public initiative, even if they try to escape paying for it. States, and the peoples they represent, thus remain powerful agencies for establishing the constitution of a market economy and for triggering – using the language of Chapter 2 – reflexive dynamics that can produce more rather than less of what they want. Some instruments are less effective than others, but that does not mean the instruments do not exist, nor that there are not very good ways to make them yet more effective still. We do have choices. And we can make them.

The Stakeholder Economy and Society

If we don't like the present, can we imagine a better future? We don't want to live in a society with 15 per cent of its adults unemployed or economically inactive, who would work if they could; we would like the figure to fall rather than rise. Equally there is no need for the incomes of the poor to decline so far beneath the incomes of the rich. We know that levels of crime are growing exponentially, especially for those at the bottom; somehow we need to stop the contagion spreading.

There need to be stronger social sanctions against the actions of errant men who through stalking, violence and even murder are terrorising, if not our lives, our imaginations – especially those of women. The increasing number of inner-city areas which are locked in downward spirals of underachievement needs to be arrested immediately – with all that that implies for housing, education and families. We do not need our civil liberties menaced and the authoritarian state strengthened as a substitute for forms of social control that have withered away under the attack of the market.

We would like better public transport. Better public facilities in the round – from universities to our health service. We need a higher investing, more innovative, more far-sighted business sector. In those areas where Britain still retains some edge, it is important that new companies come forward to take advantage of British strengths and that they do not succumb to takeover or become parts of larger monopolies. Finance should be the servant of business, not its master. The great rewards in our society should fall to those who have genuinely earned them through the risks they have run and the judgement they have exercised – not because they were born to the right parents, move in the right circles or can take percentages from deals, whether in investment banking, organised crime or selling on their interest in newly privatised companies. We like the new choice in our media, but not so much that we welcome the falling standards and the possible withering away of the BBC.

Our democracy should be more responsive to public opinion and more representative of it. But above all the British state should no longer, as we enter the twenty-first century, be above the rule of law and still substantially in thrall to the hereditary principle. Contemporary life makes redundant the notion that the majority party in the House of Commons should become, for the life of a parliament, in effect the state without any check or balance. Nothing – from freedom of assembly to the competence of local government – is therefore safe from the exercise of partisan power. Britain should develop its constitution to secure essential liberties, entrench core rights and the accompanying obligations. There must be a genuine check and balance against the House of Commons; the House of Lords needs to develop into an elected second chamber. Fixed-term parliaments should be elected with a more proportional voting system. There must be freedom of information. A code of rights must be built into British law. Decentralisation of government, and devolution to Scotland, Wales and Northern Ireland must be provided for. We must grow up.

My belief is that most, if not all, of this wish list is shared by the majority of the British. It is a demand for a more inclusive, fairer, higher-investing Britain with a well-functioning democracy. It is a vision of a stakeholder economy and society, but constructed by a contemporary state in contemporary conditions.

Stakeholding has been much mocked and maligned. If its protagonists say that they want to change British culture, they are asked how; and when they describe how either they are ridiculed for waffling or written off as trying to reinvent failed British corporatism or wanting to import the allegedly failed German social market model into Britain. In this categorisation either you are for capitalism, which can only have the shape approved of by contemporary Conservatives, those chairmen of the top 100 companies unsympathetic to change and the opinion-leaders in right-wing newspapers, or against it, so that your proposals must come from the same statist lineage as other capitalist critics over the century, and lead to the same conclusions. Both are wrong.

It is true that stakeholding is informed by the concern that unalloyed, individualistic capitalism throws up the dynamics described in the last two chapters and which have their root in the assertion of individual property rights without proper mechanisms to challenge the resulting unfair distribution of risk, of income and of opportunity. Worse, these patterns get locked in self-reinforcing dynamics of under-investment, ghettoisation, under-employment, growth of crime and all the rest which diminish everyone's lives. But the response is not to call for the socialisation of capitalism, big government or a new corporatism, rather it is to design institutions, systems and a wider architecture which creates a better economic and social balance, and with it a culture in which common humanity and the instinct to collaborate are allowed to flower.

The task is to get the institutions that lie between the state and the individual – pension funds, business firms, banks, universities, TECs, housing associations, trade unions, even satellite television stations – voluntarily to operate in ways that reflect the costs that individualist action motivated by self-interest necessarily imposes upon the rest of us. As far as possible the obligations should not be too prescriptive, which is why so much stakeholding language is cast in terms of acceptance of responsibilities as well as assertion of rights and changing the culture. If these are properly incorporated in market actors' decision-making processes, then the adverse biases in contract capitalism can be shifted. But to make real progress a government has to design incentives, make laws and create new innovative institutions which entrench such behaviour and allow for more common purpose, while trying as far as possible not to intervene directly as a market actor itself although that may be necessary. The need is for 'triggers' that can be quite modest – but which generate powerful 'multiplier' effects.

That drive needs to be supported by ensuring that individuals are not exposed to an unreasonable and unfair degree of risk, whether it is the risk of being educated poorly or dying in poverty. This is in part about not allowing inequality to spread too widely, in part about upholding and modernising systems of collective risk-sharing, notably the welfare state, and in part about ensuring opportunities for everyone to participate fully in the country's economic and social life. Because these decisions need to be taken collectively, they are intimately shaped by the structure of our democracy. The political, the economic and the social are thus interlinked into a whole; if an inclusive polity rests on political citizenship, the same inclusive rules of citizenship apply in the economic and social spheres.

Unlike 1945, the state cannot expect to establish a web of administrative bureaucracies to achieve its ends; the current world is too fluid, the competitive demands too intense, and the coalition of interests that can support such initiatives too unstable. What it has to do instead is to find points of maximum leverage on the private sector which will set in train the dynamics it wants to see, while protecting and advancing the interests of those institutions that embody the public interest.

The age of top-down blueprints has gone, if it ever existed. The state cannot plan or proscribe individual behaviour; nor in a free society should it attempt to do so. Equally the capacity for government, business and trade unions to hammer out binding deals to shape the economy and society does not exist. In a British context, with a federal union structure, weak federations of business organisations and an overpowerful but essentially disengaged state, corporatism was never very successful in its heyday; now, except for those limited areas where economic interests coincide, it is a non-starter.

Nor should the appeal to construct a stakeholder economy and society be seen as a desire to reproduce German, Swedish or Japanese capitalism in their totality in Britain – even if that were possible or desirable. The basic building blocks, ranging from powerful trade unions with a culture of working with business to a wider value system in which production and innovation are celebrated, are not sufficiently strong.

We have to start instead from where we are, with the institutions we have and in a highly open economy operating in a globalising market. Nor is it any good tinkering. We have to regard the system in its totality, looking for the linkages between the economic, social and political and trying to push the whole system in a stakeholding direction. The individual moves may be small, even cautious, as they are tested by their results, but they should be designed to produce large effects from small changes. And the effects should make sense as part of a larger strategic whole.

The Central Importance of Employment

The fulcrum around which the good society turns is an equitable distribution of work and income. The most important source of poverty and homelessness remains joblessness; the most important indicator of individual well-being is the ability to work in ways that allow you to feel that you are acting on the world in the best way that you can. To work is to gain an income, certainly; but it is to acquire skills, to win friends, to gain status, to assert your very existence. Enforced idleness is numbing; your humanity seeps through your fingers and you can feel your life ebbing away. It is no accident that the highest rates of suicide are among the unemployed. The first objective of any democratically elected government must be the promotion of work; indeed, with the cost of unemployment currently estimated at over £22 billion, lowering joblessness is an economic imperative in its own right.

But if it's work that's wanted, Conservatives respond, it's right-of-centre policies that have delivered. They are wrong. Unemployment has been disguised, as argued earlier, and job insecurity for men has risen sharply. Not only that, real wages at the bottom are falling while those at the top explode. The contract model of the labour market under the guise of 'flexibility' has allowed employers to parcel up units of labour time as a commodity like any other, so that it can be bought as part-time labour, contract labour, temporary labour and so on. But the commodity that new right economists and politicians want us to buy and sell with so little hindrance is not any commodity; it is that most precious resource, work, of central importance to our very humanity.

The policy objective, then, is to try and shape the demand for work while finding means of retaining its humanity – so that it is stopped, as far as possible, from turning into a hireable and fireable commodity. Yet the process has to respect basic economics; unless employers can change the balance of their workforces as patterns of demand change, and pay them accordingly, they confront trading losses and ultimately bankruptcy. No economy, industry or firm can operate with a prohibition on making workers redundant. On the other hand, few employers set out to treat people badly; rather they find themselves in circumstances in which, unless they lower their wage costs aggressively, the prosperity and independence of their enterprise is in jeopardy.

The Creation of an Investment Culture

The tone, objectives and culture of any private firm is set by its owners; it would be curious if this were otherwise. If company owners valued investment more and committed to their company over time, then the adverse dynamics cited above would be very much weaker. Thus paradoxically one of the first places to act upon to change the world of work is not the labour market itself, but the forces that shape the market and in particular the priorities of firms' owners.

The eccentric aspect of British capitalism is how poorly its owners discharge their responsibilities. For while the ultimate owners of most British companies may be individuals committing their life savings to pensions and insurance schemes who want the companies in which they invest to be patient and long-term in their strategies, they delegate the job of managing their ownership rights to professional investment managers. They in turn define their responsibility as being not to the company in which they invest, but to the savers who have entrusted to them their savings – whose assets they need to maximise over the shortest possible period in order to make their own business as investment managers prosper. This priority thus becomes the priority of the directors and managers of the companies in which they invest. Worse, as described in Chapter 2, the structure of institutional share ownership is such that no one investment manager can ever take responsibility for the fate of British companies; they are not large enough to be committed owner-anchors, nor small enough not to matter – thus helping to create the takeover culture. British managers of investment funds are not going to become committed family owners or patient paternalists overnight, but we need them to behave more like this than they currently do.

Fund managers are locked in a classic example of how an apparently efficient contract between two contracting parties – between them and their savers – can have disastrous spillover effects for the operation of the system as a whole. Unless the funds they manage keep up with or beat the stock market indices, then they can lose the entire account to a new firm of managers. The contract can be switched with little notice, and billions of pounds of shares can suddenly be managed by someone else. Because the firms want to keep the business and win business from others, they are forced into a position in which everyone is trying to do better than the average, which is definitionally impossible. The resulting instability helps to generate uncommitted, disengaged owners.

Two changes in the rules of the game would transform matters. The intense competitive pressures that produce such febrile behaviour need to be reduced. It should only be possible to switch between designated investment manager, every five years for funds over a certain size, say £100 million; and once any change is made, the transfer should be phased over a period of, say, three years. Ownership is a serious business, and those charged with discharging the ownership responsibilities of the bulk of British business need themselves to be given the architecture in which they can take a far-sighted view.

This needs to be backed by changes in the taxation régime. At the moment pension funds, owners of nearly 50 per cent of British business, receive their dividends tax-free – a very substantial incentive to press for the highest dividends possible. They are exempt from capital gains tax, which is paid by other investment institutions at a standard rate, whether they have held shares for twenty years or twenty minutes. No financial institution, pension fund or unit trust has an incentive to take a long-term view. If the tax treatment of dividends under advanced corporation tax was changed, and a capital gains tax was introduced for all investment institutions – including pension funds – which rewarded the long-term holding of shares, then the incentives in the system would be redirected towards increasing tomorrow's profits rather than extracting as much as possible today.

And there need to be stronger formal institutional links between institutional investors and their companies to encourage more committed ownership. At the moment investment managers receive a flood of so-called analysis about the companies they own from stockbrokers and investment banks, whose aim is to get them to buy, to sell or to do a deal.

They can use the stock market to act quickly and the commission, although tiny in percentage terms, is huge, given the vast size of the blocks of shares that subsequently change hands and on which the commission is based. The incentives are for advice to generate activity, rather than for more long-term independent knowledge about the company to inform investment decisions. Much of it, moreover, is wrong.[4]

One constructive idea, floated by the *Promoting Prosperity* report,[5] is to require all investment institutions over a certain size to form a Council of Institutional Investors (CII) to engage in high-level investment research themselves, especially of companies that worry them through their poor performance. The Council could regularly publish a list of companies in which it lacks confidence. Membership would be mandatory for any investment fund wishing to trade in the United Kingdom. So instead of companies watching their share price plunge or climb to ever more unsustainable heights, they would have a formal means of talking to their owners about their prospects. If they wanted to reorganise or restructure their companies, they could explain their plans directly and win committed support while the process was under way. And when they wanted to appoint non-executive directors to their boards who could look after investor interests but in a constructive way, the CII could also play a key role in training and supplying them.

If these measures were introduced, along with a much tougher approach by the competition authorities to the monopoly implications of takeovers, then the character of the British financial system would change in important ways. Ownership would start to become professionalised rather than being, to paraphrase Keynes's aphorism, the byproduct of a casino. The growing number of 'social investors' acting for trade unions, churches, ethical funds and so on, who already try to take their ownership responsibilities seriously, would be further strengthened. Real indicators of a company's performance would become as important as financial indicators. Takeovers would be reduced. A bias towards more long-sighted corporate behaviour would be introduced.

The City's reaction, though, can be relied upon to be

hysterical. Pension funds would insist that they were being robbed. The CII would be dismissed as a talking shop, and trusts would be set up overseas to deal in shares with bogus, nominee or false titles of ownership to avoid membership and paying contributions. Any restriction on takeover would be regarded as an inhibition on efficiency. And anyone promoting the idea that asset managers should themselves be more insulated from short-term pressures would be accused of protecting the inefficient.

Here the reforming government must hold its nerve. These are minimal requirements – the least that can be done to effect any significant change – and it should be ready with second-round initiatives to counter the reaction. Any investment house wishing to invest British savings will have to abide by the rules; if it tries to circumvent them with artificial devices then its directors should know they will be considered to be behaving illegally, subject to criminal sanction and the company's assets potentially made forfeit. Strong rules exist to prevent trade unions striking without balloting their members; a similar approach should be extended to compliance with rules in the City. Laws are made to be complied with – as much by those at the top of our society as at the bottom.

Nor can the drive to create a more investment-oriented culture stop there. British banking is notoriously weak in supporting small- and medium-sized enterprise. Decision-making is centralised, and lending conforms to rigid formulae set in London. Lending remains, despite efforts to prove the contrary, highly short term; although overdraft finance is apparently falling in importance and 'term' lending increasing, this is largely because overall loan demand is weak – and in any case 'term' loans tend to be for one year. Evidence that British business is getting the finance it requires is spurious; most businesses have no idea what finance they could and should get, or is available to their competitors overseas – so their judgement is rather like asking an anexoric if they need more food. Their answer that they don't is not to be regarded as a sign of health, any more than a British business sector reporting it is happy with short-term debt that has been secured against every movable asset in sight should be regarded as a sign that all is well. In short, Britain needs a banking system that lends long term to its growing businesses, allowing them to gear up for expansion.

Suggested remedies in the past in this area have been uniformly statist, varying from proposing a national investment bank to even nationalising the banks. A stakeholder approach is more subtle even while it recognises that there may be occasions when the state may have to design or re-design banking structures directly. What is wanted is some effective point of leverage that will produce a market dynamic towards more long-term lending – and here insolvency law and the British approach to collateral offer fertile territory. Instead of privileging banks in insolvency proceedings, so that short-term credit lines secured against a 'floating charge' of all the company's assets have pride of place in the wind up, banks should be downgraded in legal importance. More especially the practice of taking a floating charge against a company's assets, so that the bank can sell anything from the director's personal computer to the factory itself to get its money back in the event of bankruptcy, should cease. Instead the bank should have to specify what collateral it demands.

The impact, over a period of years, would be enormous. At the moment banks provide finance to companies not as going concerns, with an eye to their business prospects, but on their wind-up value. The company that gets finance has directors who will offer their houses as collateral or it has an underlying business that is rich in assets; banks like high-street retailers with prime sites rather than out-of-town manufacturers renting factory space on a trading estate or innovators on a science park. The former is bankable, the latter are high risk; but it is on the latter that the country's prosperity hangs. Banks, instead of relying on a favourable legal system to do their job for them, would have to do the legwork themselves if they wanted to lend money safely. They would have to evaluate business propositions in business rather than property terms. They would require better business plans and financial skills from their customer base, forcing more decentralisation of decision-making as hard information had to be gathered on the ground – and in turn business would learn it had to provide such information if it was to get the loans it required. Any system of regional development agencies, for example, would then work with the grain of a new decentralised financial system, helping in turn to reinforce the new local bias to decision-making and building of relationships.

Of course it would be better if Britain possessed the networks of regional banks that there are in the United States or the great regional mutual banking organisations of Germany – but we don't. Mutuality, if anything, is under assault, with the building societies turning themselves into banks. That does not mean all is lost; the banks themselves have found that operating the mutual loan-guarantee scheme, in which an insurance premium is attached to loans to small- and medium-sized businesses so that the bank can recover a high proportion of loan in the event of bankruptcy, has helped their confidence. The scheme could be vastly improved, lowering its cost to borrowers and coverage to lenders, which would give long-term lending to business a significant boost.

The objective of these stakeholder initiatives in both ownership and financing is not just to encourage higher investment; it is to give firms the financial and ownership architecture in which they can behave in a more long-term and humane fashion to their employees and wider stakeholders. The think tank Demos has floated the notion that companies should be able to reduce their tax liabilities to the extent that they offer desirable public goods like training, restrict environmentally damaging production practices and offer child care facilities and so on; while some US Democrats have developed the concept of the 'responsible corporation' which gets tax and regulatory advantages in exchange for behaving in a stakeholder fashion. Certainly if firms are to regard themselves more as trustees for a business as a social organisation than as contractors combining commodities – work, capital and technology – to maximise profits, then they will need every incentive at hand. They will also need to operate in a market where monopoly – in all its manifestations – is much more effectively policed. Stakeholding is dependent upon competitive and not monopolistic market structures.

The common thrust is to get as much decentralisation as

possible, given where we start, to build up institutions that lie between the state and individual, hence the approach to pension funds and the creation of the CII, and to construct incentives that help to create more committed ownership and more long-term bank finance, while respecting the new constraints introduced by globalisation. The objective is to build a constitution for the market whose rules impart the dynamics and culture that lead to a high-investment, high value-added economy – which we know will not occur by itself.

Unemployment and Democracy

Unemployment and poverty are geographic as much as economic and social phenomena. They are concentrated not only in our northern industrial cities and older ports, but even the more prosperous parts of the country – like London and the south-east – have areas like east London, where the desolation, social deprivation and long-term lack of work match that anywhere in the country. Unemployment is not evenly spread, any more than are employment and high wages.

As argued in Chapter 2, the reflexive character of contract capitalism demonstrates itself physically in the booming and depressed parts of the national economy by city and region. There are cities and towns, along with their catchment areas, which are caught up in a virtuous circle of growth, investment, employment generation and high wages, while others are trapped in a circle of decline. Nor is the process self-correcting by 'natural' market processes; it can last for decades. But the geographic cluster effect of growth is no accident; nor is the cluster effect of depression.

Growing firms require suppliers, and it is much easier to handle supply relationships if the contracts can be reinforced by personal interaction and trust. Thus there is a premium in having a significant part of a firm's network of sub-contractors locally based, so that sheer physical proximity and regular personal contact allow the relationship to be policed by frequent personal interaction, which is easier if the suppliers are near by. Growing firms of necessity require growing supply chains, which in turn produce a market for services of every kind – from accountancy to fast-food restaurants. Soon the whole area is in a self-reinforcing process of growth.

The same process, of course, works in reverse. Once the economic base of a city starts to wither, the knock-on consequences cascade through the supply chain and into the wider economy. Liverpool's dependency upon the static Atlantic trade is a good example of the cluster working in reverse, while the central London economy offers a textbook series of growing cluster networks: from the City itself, through the jewellery and legal districts of Hatton Garden and the Inns of Court to the new independent television and advertisement production district of Soho. All have local back-links and individual supply chains, all close to or geographically in the cluster, which help further to stimulate the local economies which they dominate.

Unemployment is too frequently analysed either as a 'macro' issue, to be tackled by 'macro' policies such as public spending or interest rates, or a 'micro' problem to be addressed by improving the functioning of the labour market – frequently little more than code, as we have discussed, for making it easier for employers to sack workers, lower their wages and restrict their rights. In truth, unemployment is partly a spatial problem. In low-wage, depressed areas it is not possible for workers to price themselves into work, or, if the local firm cluster is weak, for employment to respond very much if demand is raised nationally. Job guarantees, job subsidies and extra training work poorly in these areas, because there is not the critical mass of private- and public-sector employers to lift local employment levels materially; what is needed is the prior development of a cluster – otherwise all that state-supported employment generation becomes is a scorned government scheme organised by a derided local agency with no legitimacy and, what is worse, which is recognised to be ineffective. 'Workfare' schemes, in which unemployment benefit is made conditional on accepting any form of work, including government make-work schemes, are thus especially noxious; typically, there is no real work to be done in the travel-to-work area of the unemployed because of its geographic clustering. Workfare is thus an exercise in economic futility whose sole purpose is to reassure the advantaged that the approach to the unemployed is punitive. It is, as the Churches' Report on Unemployment and the Future of Work argues, morally repugnant and ineffective.

So, to another paradox. A precondition for a successful policy towards unemployment is a vigorous local democracy. A powerful mayor and city council will fight to establish and sustain a local cluster; they have a vested interest in the area that no one else can match. They themselves become centres of political power, whose capacity to fund projects independently and to launch local initiatives itself acts as a magnet to local business. This is the political architecture in which a local élite can act to further its own local interests, which also becomes an important precondition for the establishment of a cluster in its own right.

Already the lack of a governing authority for London is beginning to threaten the city's prosperity, most notably over the disastrous condition of public transport, where the lack of strategic direction and political voice has allowed decay and underfunding. But in those urban areas where the natural cluster base is already weak, Britain's political centralisation has exacerbated local economic weaknesses. The Training and Enterprise Councils, for example, find they do not have sufficient flexibility to address local needs, nor the clout that local legitimacy – through being democratically accountable – would give them. Worst of all they have no capacity to raise or borrow the funds that might give them real muscle.

Thus political reform, empowering cities and regions, would set in train another important dynamic – giving local communities some real leverage over their economic base. If this went in hand in hand with the initiatives over investment listed earlier, the new financial and political framework would prove an important impetus to regenerating local clusters over the country, and breathe real life into nationally devised mechanisms for lowering unemployment. Councils could use their procurement budgets to stimulate local enterprise more; more robust links could be forged between universities and the local business community; local initiatives by the new wave of 'social entrepreneurs' could expect more robust and committed backing.[6] Little by little the diminished social capital could be restored, itself an important precondition for successful enterprise. Local movers and shakers would have more influence over what happened in their own backyard, rather than having to appeal to London for help. The communities which used to run our great regional cities, which have been dismembered, demoralised and disheartened by the way the current system operates – and which are fundamental to any regeneration – would begin to be resurrected.

If this is a necessary condition for lowering unemployment, by itself it is insufficient. There have to be national initiatives. Rehiring anybody out of work for more than a year is a risky and potentially expensive task; their skills are redundant and they have lost the habit of and discipline required for regular work. Yet the benefit and training system makes no discrimination between those out of work for months, and those out of work for years; so the new hirer immediately opts for the person who has been out of work for less time, even though the wider social advantage is for the long-term unemployed person to be hired.

This rational calculus for the employer needs to be changed by offering a subsidy that rises in scale the more years the unemployed person has been out of work. In a sense this is no more than giving the firm the income support that would otherwise have been paid to the unemployed; an investment by the state in lowering long-term unemployment and in helping to prevent the long-term unemployed from staying that way. Every year a man or woman is out of work, the more likely it is they will remain out of work for a subsequent year – a disastrous waste of a life as well as a financial drag on the Treasury which could be better deployed as spending on investment. But again a job subsidy scheme of this type works best in interaction with a dynamic local community and growing business sector, hence the need for it to be combined with the other policy changes.

The Institutions of Government

There are a wide number of initiatives to be tried, but they can only get to first base if central government is itself imbued with an investment culture – and feels itself to owe an obligation to all its citizens. Here is one of the more fatal deformations of the British democratic system, certainly as it has developed within the prevailing Conservative culture; namely that public spending is a cost that brings little benefit. The proper concern of any finance ministry, that the public finances are sustainable and debt is controlled, has been turned into a fetish that public expenditure has to fall constantly as a proportion of national income, notwithstanding the impact on the citizens as a whole, or the potential returns that are available from public investment.

The British constitution is at the root of the problem. The fusion of parliament into both a law-making body and the source of government means there is little effective sanction or scrutiny of government. The first-past-the-post system of voting means that whole regions can have few or even no elected members of the governing party and so have negligible leverage over political decision-making. And the doctrine of parliamentary sovereignty means that the machinery of government ends up serving the governing party rather than any conception of the public interest. As a result, measures which have longer-term pay-backs and which benefit the wider community always struggle to win political priority over the governing party's pet projects and the interests of its supporters. This is a feature of any democracy, but Britain's structures accentuate it.

More than any other ministry, the Treasury most perfectly embodies the defects of the constitutional structure of which it is part. It sees itself in part as the instrument of the Chancellor of the day in implementing marginal annual tax and spending changes that reflect his and his party's national political priorities, and in part as the state's accountant-in-chief, making sure the books balance. There is no delegation to local or regional interests with the accompanying right to raise funds and determine spending locally (the centralised system allows for none); any concern to maximise national advantage is constantly undermined by the necessity to serve the party interest (there is no countervailing power to offset that tendency). Long-term planning is subordinated to eye-catching budgetary changes, with public investment delayed, cut or deferred because there is more immediate advantage in other current spending or tax-cutting programmes – and again there is no countervailing pressure. The Treasury seems incapable of breaking out of the one-year planning cycle for public spending, so attempting to evaluate programmes over a longer period.

Unless and until the British system of government changes, the Treasury will remain a roadblock to creative public initiative, wedded to an ideology in which the private sector supposedly creates 'wealth' which the state can then distribute according to the priorities of the governing party and exigencies of the moment. 'Welfare' is then promoted by spending or tax changes, depending on what ideology is in the ascendant. The notion that the state itself can launch and guide the motion of a market economy – which itself can have profound effects on society – is foreign to it. That would imply the Treasury has to be more than an accountant, seeing welfare essentially as how it distributes spending between government departments; instead it would have to be a policy entrepreneur taking a much more holistic view of how the economic and social interact – and how public expenditure can deliver real benefits.

The Treasury's formal power, however, is weakening. Financial decision-making is migrating to other centres – notably to the Bank of England over monetary policy, and to the European Council of Ministers over the main contours of budgetary policy. Indeed the growing power and possible independence of the Bank of England – as long as it is properly constituted – would be an important potential counterweight to the Treasury's institutional dominance. Devolution of political power to British nations, regions and cities – and with it more local power to set budgets, spend, tax and borrow – would accelerate the trend.

The blunt and crude measure of public borrowing, the Public Sector Borrowing Requirement, should be scrapped and replaced with a new measure, the General Government Financial Deficit, which allows trading enterprises in the public sector – from housing associations to the Post Office – to borrow for investment. Public spending must be genuinely planned over at least three years. All these trends and developments reinforce each other as 'triggers' to change behaviour; they promise in the long run a much healthier, and much more democratic, framework of economic policy. If the Treasury wishes to retain its role in British government, it will need to earn it.

Sharing the Risk

As argued in Chapter 2, another key component of a successful economic and social policy is the lowering of inequality, or at least its stabilisation. Inequality of income destabilises the pattern of demand, with the winner-takes-all effect seriously misallocating resources. Inequality of risk exacerbates short-termism as people compensate for uncertainty in the future by looking for ever greater returns in the present. Moreover, the social consequences of inequality have growing economic effects, as those at the bottom churn from unemployment to semi-employment and back again with little incentive to train or improve their lot. Their deteriorating family structures impose wider costs; it is society that has to pay for the consequences of broken homes and repressing criminal activity. Meanwhile, the high spending of the rich drives too many resources into the provision of private health, education and luxuries. The economy grows unbalanced, society fragments and it becomes harder to bind the classes together in a common effort as their value systems diverge.

One of the most important intermediate institutions which protects ordinary people from these trends is the most reviled, at least in the popular press: the trade unions. No account of the change in the labour market over the last fifteen to twenty years is complete without consideration of the marginalisation of trade unions and the dramatic decline in membership. In some respects the change is healthy. Trade unions, which grew up in the nineteenth century as important champions of workers' rights, demanding improvements across the whole gamut of issues and rebalancing the power relationship between business and labour, had by the 1970s collapsed into lobbies for ever higher wages, and in some cases, unjustifiable working practices without the acceptance of any parallel obligations.

However, the case against trade unions was overstated, and their role in offering a measure of protection against the powerful trends in the labour market wholly underestimated. Trade unions are needed again, not as the shock troops of the working class in building a socialist Jerusalem, but as an institutional conduit for trading off more job security and continuity of employment, for example, for lower pay increases. They can express individual workers' desire for fairer contracts between employer and worker, while policing the range of health, pensions and safety-at-work issues which concern workers, in a way that no other labour market organisation can; they act in workers' interests and, as long as they have rights of organisation and representation, are a fundamental mechanism in ensuring that some of the social and economic costs of excessive labour market flexibility are contained. They can insist, for example, that if compulsory redundancy cannot be avoided, then at least employers take the matter seriously – offering generous redundancy terms and so making sure that the costs of flexible labour markets are more equally shared between worker and employer.

In short, individual workers do need to have associations that advance their interests, and with some genuine countervailing power. The rules that disallow and obstruct unions from recruiting and being recognised need to be relaxed, and the unions need to transform themselves from monolithic bureaucracies into genuine mutual societies for the advancement of all worker interests, from ensuring the provision of banking services in disadvantage areas to offering advice on job contracts. One possibility is that they should develop more as employee mutuals, supporting individual workers over a career in different firms.[7] There is also a case for changing company law so that union representation on company boards is mandatory, along with representatives of the great savings institutions; it would force the two sides of industry into a partnership and change the dynamics of the relationship profoundly for the better.

Yet only so much can be achieved by building up intermediate institutions. There has to be a national initiative as well. After all, the best instrument both for ensuring more equality and for a reasonably financed state is a progressive tax system, in which income, wealth and consumer spending are all taxed so that the better-off pay proportionally more. The growing right-wing clamour for low 'flat-rate' taxes and for falling tax rates generally, especially on the rich, is to deny that rising inequality has any adverse economic and social impact, and to advance the controversial propositions that wealth creation is propelled solely by the prospect of individual gain, and can be reliably and fairly distributed by 'trickle-down' market mechanisms. But it is teams, organisations and cultures which lie behind wealth creation. That is not to deny the role of individual genius; it is rather to argue that making the tax system revolve around the notion that the height of the marginal rate of tax is somehow fundamental to the development of individual business genius and an enterprise culture is ridiculous. Moreover, if market processes could distribute income fairly, we would not have inequality.

Two more instruments launched at national level might help to contain inequality: a minimum wage to provide a floor for wages and measures to link directors' pay more directly to long-run business success, so introducing some form of income ceiling. Wages, as we noted in Chapter 1, are falling for lower wage earners and are forcing employers into a 'race to the bottom' in which competitive advantage in a growing number of industries depends upon bidding down wages to ever lower levels. Companies may not wish to enter the Faustian auction, but if they do not their costs will get out of line and they will lose business. Meanwhile the state's welfare payments grow as low-wage families turn to the social security system to achieve subsistence income.

Nor is this economically efficient. Turnover rates climb in the low-wage jobs, and it gets ever harder to fill vacancies with decent applicants. Quality falls, and as vacancies become protracted there is even an impact on output – firms can't produce as much if they are understaffed. But the dynamic of the market does not allow them to bid up wages; they would be forced to raise prices, and with so many firms in the market they would lose business. They are trapped.

The minimum wage is a way of springing the trap and altering the dynamic of the market. It means that there is some price below which both wages and product prices cannot fall, and so the downward vortex is arrested. But it also means that there is a wage floor, and so a preventative wedge is put into one of the drivers of inequality.

Without a maximum wage, the instruments at the top are higher rates of tax – and more discipline in the way remuneration packages are settled for directors. The device by which directors' contracts are continually rolled over on a two- or three-year basis, thus ensuring any severance pay is maximised and the share option schemes which make no differentiation between the general movement in share prices and the long-run performance of the company, are particularly noxious. Recent research shows that increasingly there is little relationship between directors' pay and company performance, and sometimes a negative relationship, so that the worse the company does, the higher the pay![8] The codes established by the Cadbury and Greenbury committees on the way companies are governed and directors paid need to be hardened and incorporated into law. Pay that is outrageous by any standards sends an important message: it says to workforces that their efforts are minor besides those of the boss-hero, especially if his or her pay simply ratchets up with a general rise in share prices; and it says to the world beyond that the super-rich have different values and codes from the rest of us. It is economically, socially and culturally divisive.

But while this argues for higher marginal tax rates, taxes should only be as high as they need to be to secure the financing of those goods which we need to deliver collectively through the state, and to redistribute such income from the rich as is needed to give the poor a reasonable standard of living in relation to the average. If that can be done in Britain with the current structure of tax rates, so much to the good; but the evidence before our eyes is that public expenditure on everything from transport to primary schools needs to be lifted. Taxes are too low; they need to be raised to halt the growth of inequality, to finance public goods like education and health and to rebalance the economy between consumption and investment.[9]

Here an important principle needs to be reaffirmed. There are certain risks that are more efficiently insured against by collective than by individual insurance. The new developments in medical technology underline the proposition; individuals can now discover, through sophisticated gene tests, what their health experience is likely to be. Already the British Association of Insurance Brokers has announced that insurers will not provide life insurance cover of more than £100,000 for anybody whose genes foretell a fatal disease. Health cover is still provided for by a tax-financed National Health Service, but if it were replaced by personal, individualised insurance then the same difficulty would reproduce itself. Full health insurance would only be available to those whose genes promised they would not need it; insurance companies, after all, don't exist to lose money.

Indeed private health insurance is so hedged about with exclusions, let-outs and ceilings over allowable expenditure that even those who hold it are increasingly aware that it provides only partial cover, which declines as they grow older and most need it. But health risk is one that is confronted by every living human being, confirming the view that the most efficient insurance is one that incorporates as large a population as possible. If we could all hold a mass conference over how best to organise health insurance, the rational course of conduct (rather than engaging in the lottery of finding out if your genes predict a good or a bad health experience and therefore whether you can obtain personal health insurance) would be to avoid the throw of the dice and enter into a collective insurance agreement which guarantees you low-cost health care whatever your future health. The job of a democratic government is to ensure that the rational course of action is adopted – and to protect individuals from individualised health insurance. Moreover, the advantage of funding the NHS from taxation is that there is an element of redistribution; the rich pay proportionately more, so helping to ensure the health of all. There plainly have to be some limits, so that removing tattoos or beautifying a nose, for example, can only be justifiable if they are demonstrably a clinical necessity, otherwise the system becomes abused and its legitimacy falls away. As David Halpern and Stuart White argue persuasively, there is a distinction between the risks we all share (what they term brute luck) and those, like smoking, where the risk has arisen from personal choice. Here there is a case for charging a premium on cigarette sales that is recycled to the NHS.[10] But the general principle stands. A good society, after all, is a healthy society and social insurance is the best means to insure against the 'brute luck' that life will deal us.

Nor should the individualistic, competitive contracting ethic be allowed to enter into the structure of health-care provision because it too throws up divisive patterns of behaviour which undermine the universal ethic that morally underpins rational health care. The famous split in the NHS between purchasers and providers, and fund-holding and non-fund-holding GPs has meant that important differences are emerging between the treatment of patients, depending on the status of their GP, the pricing policy of their local hospital for its services and its capacity to raise private finance for new investment. Health care again becomes a lottery dependent upon the structures in an individual's health district; and it is the poorer districts, with less private funding to top up health facilities and with the generally poorer health that comes with low incomes, which suffer disproportionately. Yet access to core health care is surely a basic democratic right; to deny it is a denial of citizenship.

This does not mean that the market-based health 'reforms' have to be torn up; giving GPs autonomy has had beneficial effects on their ability to secure good deals for their patients. But it does mean that the antagonistic, competitive market structures which force hospitals to maximise their 'production' of low-cost operations while avoiding anything potentially expensive need to be scrapped. Instead there need to be much more collaborative incentive structures, which emphasise investment and care driven by patients' needs rather than by financial rules. Moreover, local communities need to be given a voice in the councils of local health administration, with hospital trusts organised to incorporate the interests of the patients as stakeholders.

Similar principles must apply to education. The same three riders of the apocalypse – systematic underfunding, competitive contracting and the burgeoning private sector – are undermining the notion of a universal education system in which everyone has a stake, and where individual educational needs can be met by local structures. Class sizes in primary and secondary schools are too large for adequate teaching, and are typically twice the size of those in the private sector. Teachers' salaries have slipped markedly even as the demands on teachers have risen. School buildings, equipment and playing fields are inadequate.

The doctrine of opting out has proved pernicious in narrowing the local educational resources available to local educational authorities. In this classic competitive contracting model, school is pitched against school in a battle to win 'good' pupils who will advance it up the raw league tables, but those students left behind by the process are neglected even while the local pool of LEA schools which co-operate with each other to offer a full range of educational opportunities shrinks. This is organised mayhem, informed by a bitter dislike of local authorities and an ideological refusal to accept that market contracting has adverse spill-over effects which it itself exacerbates.

Worse, the social status and educational standing of the private schools has meant that the middle class and local élites have largely opted out of state schools, and have thus ceased to be a lobby for any improvement; indeed they are an active lobby for keeping public costs down and the system weak, thus enhancing their own children's chances of winning élite university places and the entry ticket for the winner-takes-all society beyond. The private schools have also polluted the examination system, ensuring their pupils sit exams at the easiest examination boards and insisting that papers are remarked if they fall below certain grades. Rarely can an educational structure have been designed to produce so much systematic inequality and rank unfairness.

Funding levels must be raised sharply, and directed towards

those schools in disadvantaged areas which need it most and towards primary schools, where the educational paybacks are highest. Indeed primary schools are the trigger for improving the entire system: if educational levels could be raised for every 5 to 11 year old, every comprehensive school could reach the levels so far attained only by those comprehensives with high-quality feeder schools. A £4 billion programme to lower staff-pupil ratios in primary schools, together with new buildings, would be the single most creative economic and social act of any government with potentially the most dramatic returns. To ensure full diversity within local areas, local education authorities must be given back their authority over all schools, including a fixed allocation of private school places for disadvantaged children, thus exploiting the educational resource of private schools and returning them to their original vocation – the education of the poor. LEAs themselves need to be relegitimised by a revitalised local democracy. Private schools' fiscal privileges need to be made conditional on their contribution to local educational needs and the savings invested in the state system. Comprehensive education needs to become comprehensive in the best sense, offering the full range of educational opportunity to local children in a diverse range of schools. League tables need to be organised around the value that is added in the education process, so that they do not simply reflect the catchment area of the school.

To ensure educational rigour and the proper organisation of schools and classes by specialism, there need to be setting and selection procedures based on need and merit – certainly by as late as the age of fourteen. This simple proposition, essential to any properly organised system and nearly universal in its use elsewhere in Europe, is resisted as bringing back 'grammar schools', even while the current structure means that local private schools have become *de facto* grammar schools for the middle class with the double penalty that entry has to be paid for. The objections, although understandable in terms of Britain's past, need firmly to be resisted.

At university level the best option is that they should be funded properly by increased taxation; already the élite universities are over-populated with ex-private school children, and the introduction of personal loans, charges and top-up fees will progressively deter poorer state school pupils from applying. If increased taxation is deemed impossible, then the least bad option is to introduce a graduate tax, which rises progressively as graduates' subsequent incomes rise but which is not paid at all if their income is low. The principle of rolling back state funding and introducing private finance would make universities increasingly like private schools, with Oxford and Cambridge likely to emerge as the university equivalents of Eton and Harrow – privately funded preserves for the rich. This would be an educational disaster. Britain would become a full caste society, in which the avenues to the top would be available only to the children of the better off. Not only would this be social vandalism, but it would deny the country the skills and aptitude of all those born outside the charmed circle. However imperfectly, Oxford and Cambridge still currently admit state school children; the proportion will decline the more the system is privatised. The implicit assumption would be that only those carrying the genes of the rich could expect to be able – and to be educated at a top university. It would be an abrogation of the founding principles of Western civilisation, and all to keep the income tax rate down and extend the market principle into an area where it does not belong.

And what stands for education and health, must also stand for the provision of pensions and social security payments generally. Although it is obvious that the rich can confront old age, ill health and unemployment with a greater cushion of income and savings than the poor, these risks still remain universal. The question is how the insurance of these risks is to be distributed. Is there to be a system of which everyone is a member? Or is the responsibility for risk to be shouldered by individuals alone, with some minimum floor provided for by the state?

The Conservative answer is the latter, as we see with their manifesto proposals on pensions and care for old age. Yet, as argued throughout this book, this cannot be the right universal principle with which the community should confront risk, or what Halpern and White call 'brute luck'. Once again the individual contracting model is at work, only this time spiced with an appeal for individual responsibility and a desire to roll back the state. But individualising insurance for this type of risk places the greatest burden on those whose chances of needing help are highest, who are simultaneously least able to pay satisfactory insurance premiums and will find it hardest to get reasonable cover. In *The State We're In* I estimate, for example, that to achieve a pension of £9000 a year would require individual savings of over £2000 a year for twenty-five years – beyond all but the very well-off. A recent report by the Joseph Rowntree Foundation[11] showed that the cost of insurance in just three areas of welfare – unemployment, permanent health care for long-term incapacity, and long-term care insurance – is some £900 a year for a 45-year-old married man, more than six times a one-pence increase in the standard rate of income tax. Moreover, observed the Rowntree researchers, given the uncertainty over long-term care costs and needs, most policies had so many exclusions and let-outs that they would be poor guarantees in retirement in any case. And of course the poor would pay disproportionately more of their incomes for any given policy. Individualisation of insurance is a means of redistributing from the poor to the rich.

So the disadvantaged, unable to afford proper individual insurance for health, unemployment and old age, will be forced to rely on the minimum floor, which because the middle and upper classes have no stake in the system and do not contribute to it will be lower than it would have been had the system remained organised around collective insurance. This lowers social security payments, certainly, but it redistributes risk to those least able to bear it. The right present this as a moral good, because the poor and single parents alike need to be incentivised not to live off the state, and so take responsibility for their own lives. But there is a contrary moral argument. The better-off, by shifting risk to the weaker, deny their own humanity and their reciprocal moral responsibility to the community of which they are part – and which allows them freely to exercise their wealth. Worse, they actively contribute to inequality, whose growth menaces the good society from which they benefit and whose disintegration brings forth authoritarian, repressive legislation that ultimately menaces their own civil liberties. The moral argument and self-interest point in the same direction: it is in the rich's interest to uphold universal social insurance and the welfare state. Here the British political system interacts again with the dynamics of class, culture and society; it is because the Conservative party has so easily dominated the House of Commons, with a minority of the vote under a first-past-the-post system, that it has been able to organise policies with such a systematic bias towards the middle class and comfortable who have been all they needed to elect them. If governing coalitions had to be constructed from a wider constituency, the better-off would have been forced into recognising that they could not pursue their own interests so one-sidedly, and politics and policy would have been different.

These then are the building blocks with which to construct a stakeholder economy and society. The creation of an investment culture and more democratic autonomy is aimed at bringing more economic dynamism to all the country, while a proper system of distributing and sharing risk underwrites a more inclusive society. Many of the initiatives can be launched by a nation state even in today's so-called global market. However, it is becoming increasingly difficult to hold the line. To do that the country needs to look for allies, and there are fourteen of them across the Channel. Enter the argument over Europe.

4
AND SO TO EUROPE

THE EUROPEAN ISSUE has haunted British politics ever since the foundation of the European Community; it first split the Labour party and now it is splitting the Conservatives. Mrs Thatcher, declaring her implacable opposition to further European integration, triggered the loss of her premiership over the issue – the most famous casualty in a long line of British politicians who owe their political demise to Europe. But since then the Maastricht Treaties for Political, Economic and Monetary Union have raised the stakes still higher, and few readers of this book will not be familiar with the litany of arguments. Beneath the fierce exchanges over the economic merits of the single currency and allegedly looming danger of a federalist super-state, lie fundamental questions not merely about sovereignty but about the character and direction of the British as a nation. It gets very raw. For the sceptics, pro-Europeans are Quislings throwing away a thousand years of history for a political project which is essentially German, even Nazi, in its roots.[1] For the enthusiasts, Britain is allowing unreal romanticism to obstruct the prosecution of her interests, which must lie with the continent of which she is part, and once again risks missing the opportunity fully to shape it at a decisive moment.

Yet, as I argued in Chapter 1, Euro-scepticism has now become an essential component of current Conservatism's ideological worldview – bound up with defence of the unwritten constitution and British-style free-market capitalism. It is political territory where instincts and prejudice rule and reason is of little use. But behind the sound and fury, lie profoundly different trajectories for Britain's future. If Euroscepticism is intimately integral to a British political project which entails a deepening of individualistic contract capitalism, the contrary argument is also true. The stakeholder economy and society are related to if not identical with the European economic and social model, and it is easier to build and sustain them in a wider European context than acting alone. Whether it is a stimulatory economic policy to tighten the labour market – one of the best ways of countering job insecurity – or protecting the idea of collective social insurance, the policies are better executed if other European states are trying to do the same rather than engaging in competitive deflation or a Dutch auction to reduce the welfare state. Hence the case for Europe-wide economic policies and the Social Chapter alike. Europe offers policy options and an umbrella, under which policy can be co-ordinated, not available to a single state acting alone.

Conservative Euro-sceptics do not want to make these choices. Indeed they mock the European economy for miring itself in a corporatism and welfarism from which Britain has escaped. Under the guise of preserving British sovereignty and the British economic miracle the sceptics insist that the integration process be frozen and that Britain repatriate crucial powers back to London from Brussels – they generally stop short of advocating withdrawal, at least for the present. But this so-called 'regaining' of political sovereignty entails a loss of economic options for governments which have different ambitions than theirs.

British Euro-sceptics thus peddle a half-truth, bordering on a lie. They insist that they want to assert British sovereignty, but the sovereignty that they ardently desire is no true sovereignty. Rather it is to cement Britain on the course that has been set since 1979, and to deny British governments of other political hues the choices that they might want to make over the country's direction. Whether it is defence, where there are substantial savings and strategic advantages to be had from closer European integration, or conserving fish stocks in the North Sea by being inside the common fisheries policy, a decision to have a looser association or withdraw with the European Union closes down options for future governments.

Not so, retort the sceptics; there can still be collaboration in these areas, but it must be between sovereign nation states and involve no ceding of power to a European supranational authority. Withdrawal or a looser association does not mean European isolation; it means redrawing the terms of collaboration to preserve political sovereignty. But they are wrong. Their proposals would damage British economic interests, and involve a false definition of how political sovereignty can be exercised in modern conditions.

The argument over fish is a classic of the genre. Fish stocks in the North Sea are dangerously low; systematic overfishing has to be countered otherwise there will be no fish. How to divide a reduced catch between European states with fishing interests is thus both an imperative and highly political task – and it has to be international because fish swim. They do not acknowledge political boundaries. Euro-sceptics argue that Britain would get a better deal by being outside the EU, and bargaining aggressively as a sovereign nation state, but that neglects the determination of other European countries to act within the EU. Once they continue to act together and decide what the overall North Sea catch should be and how it would be divided, they would present Britain with a done deal. If Britain did not choose to accept it, we would find the combined navies of the EU protecting the EU decision, and it is hard to imagine that the British fish quota would be higher rather than lower once it was outside the horse-trading forum of Brussels. Isolation would make Britain a loser, and confront us with a combined European coalition, the very outcome Britain has tried to avoid since the sixteenth century. This is, to say the least, not especially clever.

Yet the difficulty for pro-Europeans is that the next phase of European integration is hazardous, and it is not clear that the blueprint set out in the Maastricht Treaties is achievable within the timescale allowed. The single currency is the flashpoint, with sceptics being able to marshal some apparently powerful arguments. The countries who are members of the European Union are not necessarily those who would form an optimum currency area, they say, which necessarily needs some conformity of economic and social institutions beyond convergence in key economic statistics. There are deep differences in European cultures which go far beyond narrow economic convergence – ranging from the structure of the housing markets to the way the pension systems are organised – all of which have the capacity to destabilise the process of monetary union. Currency changes are themselves important sources of adjustment, and this shock-absorber capacity, even more important when economic structures vary so much, would be frozen for good once the euro was launched. If that means of adjustment is denied, then there have to be fiscal transfers between countries to compensate for varying degrees of unemployment that the EU is not currently equipped to make on the scale required. And last but not least, if the euro is to be sustainable then no one country can abuse it by issuing more euro debt than the others. As a result there has to be close co-ordination and surveillance of fiscal policy across the Continent, and the instrument proposed – the so-called stability pact, complete with fines for countries whose policies do not conform with Conservative targets for borrowing and inflation – has a deflationary bias and entails loss of control of ultimate national economic policy to the European Council of Ministers. These are arguments with force.

The deeper problem is that Europe's political structures are so far underdeveloped in relation to its economic ambitions – and are difficult to develop further given that the peoples of the European Union do not yet share a common cultural and political consciousness. There are not pan-European political parties campaigning on issues that make pan-European sense, and until there are political institutions like the European parliament presuppose a wider political reality that does not yet exist. It is not realistic to argue, for example, that the accountability of the European Central Bank (ECB) to the European parliament as it is currently organised answers the question of the ECB's lack of political legitimacy. The parliament is simply not credible for such a task.

But here the battle-lines are drawn. For the great stimulus to bringing the European parliament alive and accord it credibility would be to give it real power, such as monitoring Europe's central bank – and an equal stimulus to creating a pan-European political consciousness would be the possession of a common currency used by all Europeans. A single currency is thus not just about lowering the transaction costs of doing business in Europe; it will set in train an integrative dynamic, which is just what the sceptics are pledged to avoid. They may complain that European institutions are ineffective or politically illegitimate; but at bottom they do not want them to be different. They do not buy the case for integration.

Yet in today's world, and the way it promises to develop in future, full membership of a more closely integrated European Union complete with a single currency and a more closely co-ordinated defence structure offers British governments leverage over economic and social events that they would not have by going alone. Indeed the paradox is that, given the subsidiarity rules within the EU, there would be nothing to stop a British government from pitching its policies at the low tax, free market end of the spectrum if it chose, the argument made by a Conservative pro-European like Kenneth Clarke.[2] Inward investment, another important prop of Conservative economic policies, is also advanced by EU membership. But for pure sceptics this pragmatism is inadmissible. The nation state should remain the foundation of the European political system, whatever the functional and political reasons for creating an ever stronger supranational authority.

Pitched at this level, the division is fundamental. There is no point in playing a role in constructing a European constitution or creating a single currency or even addressing the problems listed above. The attempt should not be made on the *a priori* grounds that it offends a key principle that nations should not cede sovereignty – whatever the gains and however tattered the sovereignty. On this there can be no compromise.

Yet the compromise has already been made, by forces beyond Britain's control. The nation state is not the best locus for international action any more; it is being circumvented and undermined whether it is by the need to conserve fish stocks, ensure the solvency of investment banks, buy weapon systems or prevent multinationals from undermining common welfare policies. If we are to relegitimise the political process, then political authority has to mean effective political action, and that must mean acting collaboratively across borders. That in turn means inventing democratic structures and electorates that extend across borders as well so that action has democratic legitimacy. We don't send cavalry into supranational battle any more on horses – they use the internal combustion engine. The times are changing.

And although British criticism of the single currency is unrelenting, there is more scope for the euro to succeed than the British consensus accepts – and important reasons why it should be made to succeed. It is true as the sceptics argue that European economic and social structures vary, but what unites European states is as striking as their differences. There is a broad European model. There is a commitment to an inclusive social security system, public health and education systems funded from progressive taxation of incomes in all European states, including Britain. All may have powerful banking systems and less dominant stock markets than Britain, and all run systems in which property rights are tempered by obligations. But that balance helps to create more far-sighted companies, higher investment and more productivity, something which Britain should aim to emulate rather than dismiss, and which this book offers some ideas about how to achieve.

European labour markets are more regulated; but taken in the round, levels of unemployment and economic inactivity are not materially higher than in Britain – and in some cases they are lower. The Europeans try to avoid pushing too much risk on to the disadvantaged, to uphold welfare systems, to sustain public goods like education and health and to run a more productivist, higher investing capitalism. I submit that these preferences are those the British would want to make if allowed to express their views free from the hysterical anti-European propaganda – and that they can make them better within the EU than outside it. The euro, if successful, enlarges the capacity to make this choice. In the first place it is likely to be a hard currency. The world's investment and financial community holds too many dollars and wants to diversify, but neither the mark nor yen can take the strain: if they are forced too high on the foreign exchange markets, then they throttle the German and Japanese economies and cause a subsequent devaluation. By contrast the euro is backed by an European economy which runs a trade surplus and is substantially self-sufficient; moreover, it will be launched, if it starts in 1999, against a background of low inflation, high unemployment and output well below potential. There will be a clamour to buy it, and it will appreciate against both the yen and dollar.

So while at the moment European investment is depressed by uncertainty over future currency arrangements, once the euro begins that uncertainty will necessarily be reduced. Moreover, the hard euro will bring to countries like France much lower interest rates than they have typically experienced, thus making investment – and borrowing for consumption – more attractive. The low-interest-rate régime will lead to an increase in asset values from houses to shares which can be expected to be permanent precisely because of the new régime; that increase in wealth will help create a Continent-wide feel-good factor, helped by the hard euro making imports cheaper and thus real incomes higher. In short the euro could be the trigger for moving Europe into a virtuous economic circle of rising investment, consumption and employment – a millennial boom.

Britain will benefit from the backwash of this recovery, but it would do better by being in rather than out. The monetary and fiscal policies of the Europeans will become the benchmark by which the British are judged; our economic policies will have to track the EU's in terms of inflation targets, projected budget deficits and scale of monetary growth, but without having any capacity to influence the decision-making or the protection of European institutions in delivering the policies. Moreover, given the size and liquidity of the London financial markets, British governments will face an unhappy asymmetry of risk; if there are doubts about the sustainability of British policy, the very powerful financial markets will react very fiercely and to more damaging effect. Thus economic policy will not only have to shadow that within the EU, it will have to be still more conservative to maintain the financial markets' confidence; interest rates will on average be higher and budget deficits lower. Sovereignty will have been reduced.

The sceptics' concern about the accompanying inability to make big intra-European fiscal transfers is rooted in the fear that the system will fail; there is no compensating optimism about the results of the system succeeding – and how that alone will put member countries' fiscal policy on a sustainable basis again, raising the tax base and lowering public spending, which will make individual welfare systems affordable. The gain is thus the protection of the European social model, surely offsetting the concern at the low scale of fiscal transfers between states over the economic cycle. Such an advantage is rarely, if ever, mentioned.

But the advantages do not cease here. The euro will also be the umbrella under which individual countries can make many more real choices over the levels of public spending and taxation, free from the veto of the financial markets and subject only to the demand from other European countries that they do not borrow more than their fair share of European savings – the underlying rationale for the much criticised stability pact. Moreover, it will put in place the first effective pan-European institutions for running the European economy as one economy, thereby breaking the hegemony of the capital markets and their veto over expansionary economic policy. Here at last is a potential means of recovering a measure of demand management, a crucial tool in the policy locker of any state.

It will also give the Europeans countervailing power over American financial policy, which has been organised up to now around a policy of benign neglect of the dollar which is favourable solely to the US economy. Successive dollar devaluations have in effect exported American unemployment to Europe, which has then been blamed on 'sclerotic', 'over-regulated' European labour markets. But with a world currency to rival the dollar, the Europeans place in their hands an instrument that can force the Americans to run their economy more soberly – and compel them to adopt a more collaborative approach in the management of the international economy, and the international institutions. The IMF, World

Bank and United Nations will want euros as much or even more than they want dollars, and this will give Europe as much leverage over these institutions as the Americans now have. There are losses to be borne by losing the capacity for individual European currencies to adjust once they lock into the euro, but they are offset by the important gains that the euro will bring to the whole international financial system.

Equally important, this is the basis of an economic and political framework which will allow medium-sized European powers to protect their unique economic and social models. The financial pressure to attack European welfare structures and labour markets will be eased, and the boom will improve the underlying fiscal position of member countries. The power relationship with multinationals and capital markets will be tilted in favour of European states, so easing the degree to which globalisation disempowers them. The single currency, in short, could be a potential master-stroke.

But it will entail a loss of formal political sovereignty to European institutions. One objection is that the European Central Bank is unaccountable and undemocratic, but this is too despairing an assessment. The central bank governors who will be appointed to its governing council are all responsible to their national governments, and the ECB itself will have to justify its action to the European Council of Finance Ministers and the European parliament. The European parliament cannot be viewed as it now is, but rather what it will become under the dynamic of managing the euro. We will all care about the interest rates set in Frankfurt.

The mechanisms for accountability thus exist at both national and European levels. Nor will decision-making solely be dominated by the desire to promote price stability; the relevant clause in the Maastricht Treaty is qualified by the need for the ECB to take employment and growth into account in its deliberations. There is also the brutal fact that monetary policy is largely semi-automatic; there is rarely little choice for democratic politicians about the direction of interest rates once they have set the wider objectives of monetary policy. The debate is remarkably technocratic, focusing generally on the timing and scale of interest rate changes rather than the direction, which is determined technically by where the economy is in the economic cycle. Once the wider objectives are set, the worries about lack of accountability are overdone.

Yet to join the single currency, to share in its benefits and play a role in its governance, undoubtedly involves a commitment to more European integration and a challenge to the old British ways of doing things. Amen to that; although the sceptics are right to say that the decision is so momentous it should be backed by a referendum. Nor is it in British interests for the euro to fail. If that happened, then the European cause could be set back seriously, perhaps even irretrievably, and British interests would be damaged thereby. All the potential gains listed above would be lost, and Europe would risk imploding into economic and political rivalries.

Yet no serious economist can evaluate the prospects for the euro with anything but caution, as a good survey by Professor David Currie for the Economist Intelligence Unit underlines.[3] While success is more likely than the British economic establishment concedes, there remains a chance that it could become an inflexible straitjacket locking Europe into excessive deflation. But if it were to succeed the benefits would be seismic. It would not just be a European economic dynamic that would be unleashed, but a favourable political one. With a single currency acting as an emerging shared European political fact, institutions like the European parliament would have more meaning, allowing them to win a vital new legitimacy. That in turn would intensify the potential to accelerate defence and foreign policy integration, held up by understandable but increasingly outdated concerns about ceding crucial areas of national interest to a supranational power. Demos estimates that reducing Europe's armies from two million to three quarters of a million in a common army would save Britain as much as £15 billion a year by the pro-rata reduction of the British defence budget[4] – savings that could be profitably deployed elsewhere.

It may be objected that Britain's interests are global rather than European, but it is a self-serving, Euro-sceptical argument. In the first place Britain's geography, culture and economic interests place us firmly as a European power; our exports to Holland exceed those to the whole of south-east Asia. Nor does European integration exclude looking outward to the rest of the globe; in a sense the two are interconnected. A better integrated and self-confident Europe, which has found ways of making supranational governance work, is a trail-blazer for the kind of international collaboration and government that will be needed more, not less, over the next century. It can operate as a model and a market, offering the rest of the world an even more secure platform in the European continent than it does at present. If the EU buckles or implodes, the hope of stabilising and integrating Eastern Europe into Western councils and the larger world economy will disappear.

Nor is European integration a German plot to take over Europe, as the sceptics increasingly allege, echoing Nicholas Ridley's comments which forced his resignation. It is true that Germany pushes for integration, but Europe is lucky both that its largest state is so pro-European and that its constitution so rigorously entrenches democracy and the rule of law. The true horror would be a Germany run according to the precepts of British Euro-sceptics – a nation state that jealously guards its sovereignty and bargains as hard as it can to prosecute its economic interests. It would force Europe into a centre organised around Germany and its satellite states, with the outlying states trying to organise constantly shifting alliances to balance German power. It would be a return to nineteenth-century balance-of-power politics, in which Britain would be cast as the permanent loser.

Britain cannot turn its back on such possibilities and neglect what is happening on mainland Europe, pretending that we are like England under Pitt – that we can survive, even prosper, as a result of a continental blockade. We cannot avoid but engage ourselves with Europe, and want its initiatives to succeed. Whether on defence or currency issues, we hold more in common with fellow Europeans than we do in opposition and we can benefit hugely from collaboration. Indeed European integration is a reflexive dynamic which empowers rather than enfeebles those who engage in it. To leave or to place ourselves on a trajectory in which departure from the EU would become inevitable would be a regression to an idea of the past that has long since evaporated. Europe is the future; the sea-faring imperial island an image that is receding ever more rapidly into a romanticised, but dead, past.

5
CONCLUSION

THE BRITISH HAVE no reason to be pessimistic. There is a good chance that after a century of experimentation between rival economic and social models we are near to finding one that might work. It will not be the individualistic contract capitalism of the Thatcher and Major years, nor will it be the corporatism of the years before or an import from abroad. If we are determined, and with a little luck, Britain could develop its own specific capitalist model, in which market flexibilities are integrated into webs of trust and commitment, and where society acknowledges the imperative of sharing risk and income as fairly as possible.

It will not be easy. Many of the 'reforms' of the Conservative years have been designed as irreversible. An opted-out business and professional class now exists in whom the merits of a harsh market individualism, which so uniquely benefits them, have been deeply instilled. Other values – of public service, altruism, justice and even fair play – have withered. The task of rebuilding public institutions and structures and of changing the British business culture is immense. It is now almost second nature to distrust any form of public initiative. We are consumers rather than investors and the belief that we cannot alter our fate has been drilled into us.

But there are alternatives. The word stakeholding has become so loaded with ambiguity and baggage that the intent behind it is overlooked. It is based in the notion that the same values that animate us to make our personal relationships work should also animate our wider economic and social relationships, that the idea we are 'soft' at home but 'hard' at work is inadmissible. The same values should inform all our dealings.

In the preceding pages I have attempted to flesh out what this might mean in practice. The design and constitution of our society's intermediate institutions, whether pension funds or trade unions, are of fundamental importance in building social capital and sustaining relationships based on trust and commitment which can encompass our conduct at work and play. If we want far-sighted firms, a modern welfare state and solid public services, they will not emerge out of thin air; they need to be embedded in the institutions and patterns of incentive which sustain them – the most important being a political system which is of the people rather than above them. If there are to be properly funded systems to underwrite the brute risks which we all face – an essential component of any just society – they need to be installed and run by a democracy which itself incorporates these values. Britain must, in short, become a polity of properly enfranchised citizens which itself is subject to a constitution of law. In this sense political, economic and social reform go hand in hand: success depends on moving on all fronts.

If this is our aim, it is clear that the Conservative party is not the instrument through which this will be achieved. It may alter its view in the future, but at present it denies that there needs to be a change of course. It is intent on furthering market individualism to the extent that it is no longer ridiculous to write in terms of it wanting to privatise the state. It is careless of the liberties it has removed as it acts to stem the mounting social disintegration resulting from the marketisation of the society it has sponsored. Some Conservatives are not blind to the vicious inequality and unfairness of contemporary Britain, but the ideology of the party's majority forbids any constructive intervention. It defends the current British constitution to the last; it is terminally suspicious of Europe. It is incapable of addressing the short-termism and under-investment that plague the public and private sectors alike. Its mission – the abandonment of British corporatism, the lowering of trade union power and the assault on nationalised industries – is complete. It is time to move on.

The question is whether in government the Labour party will seize the opportunity that is open to it. The paradox of the moment is that while Conservatism and its works may be deplored by most of the electorate (if the opinion polls are any guide), Conservative philosophy still remains in the ascendant. There may be talk of new Keynesian economics, of stakeholding, of communitarianism and so on, but there is little confidence in spelling out what these imply in terms of concrete policies. The dominant discourse of political debate still prohibits the advocacy of public spending and higher taxes, however modest; the reorganisation of company law to help stakeholder companies is portrayed as 'corporatist'; and while the language of rights and responsibilities which characterises communitarianism can be applied to the poor, to justify what are effectively workfare schemes, there is general dismay if the same principles are extended to the rich. New Labour has yet to be as brave in advocating what it is as it has been in explaining what it is not. The intellectual hegemony of Conservatism remains in place.

But it is cracking, and one of the first fruits of the Conservative party's electoral defeat – if that happens – will be a recapturing of the language of political exchange. Indeed, after eighteen years of one governing party wedded to a very particular political philosophy, it is difficult to imagine how enabling it will be to have different voices, representing a different tradition and with more rounded objectives, in positions of political authority. This alone will expose the increasingly narrow tramlines of current Conservative thought.

The risk, however, is that New Labour will remain imprisoned by the ideas it has learned to ape, and will govern too much within the parameters laid down by its predecessors. Few people advocate substantial or unwarranted increases in public spending and taxation, but it needs to be repeated that some of the best instruments available to governments to fight inequality, poverty and social marginalisation are public expenditure and higher rates of income tax. Public goods like education, health and transport cannot be provided without public spending. In this respect Richard Crosland was right. Labour's commitment to freeze income tax rates over the life of the next parliament and continue with impossibly tight targets for the growth of public expenditure for the first two years is understandable in terms of political positioning; but it means that one of the core elements of a social democratic programme has been jettisoned. Taxes can still be raised outside income tax, but they are not as effective in tackling inequality; and spending may be lifted in the later years of the parliament. But the losses cannot be regained; any growth will be from a still lower base point, involving an even seedier, more rundown public infrastructure, before there will be any relief. In this respect both the Liberal Democrats, pledged to increases in taxation to finance higher education spending, and the old Conservative 'One Nation' tradition look better defenders of public service and social cohesion than their Labour rivals.

Nor is that all. The commitments on public spending have important implications for the state as the sponsor of collective insurance against the risks we all confront. We should not be concerned if the social insurance component of public expenditure rises, unless it is driven by fraud; that is part of the contract between the government and the people and is the most economically and socially efficient means of discharging the insurance obligation. But if public spending is to grow no more rapidly under Labour than under the Conservatives, then the role of the state as risk-sharer and risk-underwriter is grievously constrained. The dynamics of contract capitalism – in thrusting unfair amounts of risk on to the disadvantaged – cannot be seriously altered or ameliorated. There is a real danger that inequality, whose presence is the overwhelming social and psychological fact of the late 1990s, may go unchecked.

And while it is right to insist that rights should be balanced by obligations, the application must be universal. There is a dangerous tendency for obligations – to search for work, to save for pensions and so on – to be imposed upon the poor, while rights – to enjoy low marginal rates of tax, to opt out into privileged private education – are voluntarily exercised by the rich. This unfairness, if it becomes general, is inadmissible and if carried to extremes it will undermine the bonds that hold society together. Labour's flirtation with a partial implementation of the rights and obligations framework, hitting the poor harder than the advantaged, is dangerous. Moral principles are universal or they are not moral.

Similarly it is all too easy, with Britain's unwritten constitution, for the imposition of obligations to merge into an unpleasant authoritarianism which undermines basic civil liberties. There is a thin line, for example, between the curfew on a council estate that protects the common good and the curfew that bans lawful assembly; between the proper punishment of offenders and care for victims and the erosion of trial by jury. The battery of measures introduced by the Home Secretary, Michael Howard, and supported by his Shadow Jack Straw – ranging from the Police Bill to the treatment of young criminals – has too frequently toppled over the line. Liberty is indivisible.

While concerns about Labour's lack of a philosophic anchor and sense of a political project are considerable, if there is one lesson to be learnt from the great ideological battles of the past it is that political projects informed by some utopian vision – some final economic and social equilibrium which can be legislated for by a sovereign parliament –are doomed. Utopias, either of the free market or socialism, never arrive. Democratic government is a much more serious affair than simply battling over such visions: it is about the business of argument; initiating processes; building institutions; creating a culture; putting in place obligations to balance the privileges of the various interest groups that constitute society; delegating, as much as possible, decisions to the local arena; and building a consensus for action.

It is true that Britain's political institutions and traditions are not built around such a conception of democracy, which is why constitutional change is essential both in its own right and as a precondition for wider economic and social reform. Britain's system of government, as Tom Paine argued so vividly two hundred years ago, is at heart a democratic masquerade. It is bound by no rules, laws or constitution so that parliament is above the law – and it governs in the same way, above the people rather than engaging with them except during general elections, which are the one occasion when the system opens up. Paine traced Britain's political institutions to the Norman invasion, an argument which seems fanciful in 1997; but there is still substance in the idea that British political structures remain more for the use of a governing, almost occupying, élite than for the people. They have certainly favoured the Conservative cause over this century.

Labour's commitment to constitutional change, the most serious package advocated by any political party since before the First World War, is thus a dramatically radical statement. It is serving notice that by wanting to change the democratic system, it wants to change the substance of democratic debate and thereby its own role in the political process. It is no longer the champion of some Labourist blueprint, which it aims to impose upon society through a parliamentary majority whatever its merits. Rather it aims to set up a democratic polity in which it will argue for the socialist ethics that govern it as a party – of equality, fairness, universalism, solidarity, political liberty, the need for public action – but within an architecture which demands continual engagement with the people over the consequence of the laws and policies that emerge from these principles. Hence the case for a revising second chamber not based on the hereditary principle; the case for a more proportional voting system; the case for more devolution and entrenchment of local democracy; the case for incorporating the European Convention on Human Rights into British law.

The establishment of a democracy which functions better opens the way to the stakeholder economy and society. The object is to build a constitution for a market economy in which firms are higher investing, more far-sighted and can build better trust relationships with their workforces, suppliers and owners. This is in part about legislation and incentives, as outlined in the previous chapter; in part about a change in the wider economic and social system so that risk is more firmly shared, thus generating more confidence and less insecurity; and in part about the cultural change that will ensue as the nature of the British state and democracy themselves change.

Seen through this prism, some common misgivings and criticisms of the Labour party's programme are misdirected. It should not be accused of lacking legislative blueprints; rather the assessment should be whether there is enough in the programme to launch the necessary dynamics – whether on stakeholding or on democracy. Here the answer is a qualified yes, qualified by the concerns raised earlier but positive none the less. For it is not a completely empty political vessel without aims. The party has identified 'trigger points', whether the role of primary schools or the composition of the House of Lords, that could change Britain substantially – and for quite modest expenditure. In the labour market, for example, trade unions will be strengthened in their capacity to represent workers and there will be a minimum wage. Even if there is nothing more than a change to the capital gains tax régime and the launch of closer links between institutional shareholders and British companies, that will trigger important 'reflexive' changes in a stakeholding direction and encourage more initiatives thereafter. The welfare state will, in principle, be sustained, and universalism protected as much as possible. The regulation of privatised utilities will be improved. There will be a change of course, however tentative.

Thus from modest beginnings Mr Blair and his party have a chance of changing the structures of British democracy, sustaining the welfare state, lowering unemployment and creating a stakeholder business culture. Moreover, to do this in such a conservative country would be no mean achievement – and here there is a seismic shift under way that is not commonly recognised.

In pre-agreeing the outlines of a programme of constitutional change with the Liberal Democrats to be implemented over the next parliament and the principles which should underpin it, Labour has both widened its political base – and again shown that it means business when it talks about creating a new British democratic culture. But something even more important is afoot. Agreement with the Liberal Democrats is part of the construction of a wider coalition of interests as Labour breaks out of its historic laager as the standard bearer of the organised working class. The best in the English liberal tradition – reformist, fair-minded, tolerant, even 'stakeholder' – is being reawakened. Moreover, it is coalescing in the formation of a new political base, extending from stakeholder, pro-European companies through the liberal professions to partnership-minded trade unions and incorporating the public sector, and bound together by near-universal support from the Christian churches and other religious traditions. This is a new formulation of Middle England, which could underpin a progressive political coalition for decades, rather as it did in the nineteenth century.

In short the country stands on the threshold of a new course which could lead it to become the most dynamic economy and healthy society in Europe. The choice must not be funked – either in the polling booth this spring, or in the months and years afterwards. There are choices to be made over the kind of market economy we live in and society we share. We can look to our rulers to initiate the changes, but in the last resort it is our responsibility to make sure they deliver. If we want a better political, economic and social order, it is there for the taking. It is, in the truest sense, up to us.

Notes and References

1 The Strange Rebirth of Liberal England

1 Taxation has risen from 34·3 per cent of GDP in 1978–9 to 35·7 per cent in 1995–6.
2 Bob Kuttner, *Everything for Sale* (Knopf, 1997).
3 See Table 1 in Ray Barrell and Nigel Pain, 'EU: An Attractive Investment', *New Economy*, vol. 4, issue 1 (IPPR, Spring 1997), p. 50.
4 The Employment Policy Institute's 'wide' measure of unemployment, U3, states that in the autumn of 1996 unemployment and economic inactivity stood at 4·4 million.
5 See Paul Gregg and Stephen Machin, *Blighted Lives* (Centre for Economic Performance, LSE, 1997).
6 Correlli Barnett's *The Long Victory* (Macmillan, 1995) is one example. Another is Andrew Roberts, *Eminent Churchillians* (Penguin, 1995).
7 Institute of Public Policy Research, *Promoting Prosperity: A Business Agenda for Britain* (Vintage, 1997).
8 See Wendy Hall and Stuart Weir, 'The Untouchables: Power and Accountability in the Quango State', *Democratic Audit*, paper no. 8 (Scarman Trust and Human Rights Centre, University of Essex, July 1996).

2 Why Markets Go Wrong

1 *Independent on Sunday* (24 December 1995).
2 *Making Connections: UK Roundtable on Sustainable Development* (February 1997).
3 George Soros, *The Alchemy of Finance* (John Wiley,

1997).

4 George Soros, 'The Capitalist Threat', *Atlantic Monthly* (February 1997).

5 Anthony Giddens, *Beyond Left and Right* (Polity Press, 1995).

6 A good survey of contract theory can be found in Oliver Hart, *Firms, Contracts and Financial Structure* (Oxford University Press, 1995).

7 Francis Fukuyama, *Trust: The Social Virtues and the Creation of Prosperity* (Hamish Hamilton, 1995).

8 Robert Putnam, *Making Democracy Work* (Princeton University Press, 1993).

9 Robert H. Frank and Philip J. Cook, *The Winner Take All Society* (Free Press, 1996). A good summary is available from the Employment Policy Institute, *Economic Report*, vol. 10, no. 10 (February 1997).

10 Sarah Jarvis and Stephen Jenkins, 'Changing Places – Income Mobility and Poverty Dynamics in Britain' (Working Paper 96-19: ESRC Research Centre on Micro-Social Change at the University of Essex, 1996).

11 *Employment Audit*, issue 2 (Employment Policy Institute, Autumn 1996).

12 Audit Commission, *Misspent Youth* (HMSO, December 1996).

13 David Smith, *Job Insecurity vs Labour Market Flexibility: The Social Market Foundation* (February 1997).

14 All figures are from *Employment Audit*.

15 Dan Corry, 'Should We Continue with a Deregulated Labour Market?', *Renewal*, vol. 5, no. 1 (February 1997).

16 Peter Robinson, 'Controversy: Evolution not Revolution', *New Economy*, vol. 2, no. 3 (IPPR, Autumn 1995).

17 See Table 3 in Stephen Bond and Tim Jenkinson, 'Investment Performance and Policy'. *Oxford Review of Economic Policy*, vol. 12, no. 2 (Summer 1996).

18 Professor Ivan Yates, 'Government Finance and Industry; Making Sense of Creating Wealth', the Marlow Lecture, October 1996.

19 IPPR, *Promoting Prosperity: A Business Agenda for Britain* (Vintage, 1997), p. 25.

20 Colin Mayer, *The City and Corporate Performance: Condemned or Exonerated?* (School of Management Studies, Oxford, December 1996).
21 See *Lombard Street Economic Research Review* (January 1997); also *Will Hutton and the Stakeholder Society* (IEA Health and Welfare Unit, 1997).
22 See Professor Tim Congdon's attack on me in the *Lombard Street Research Monthly* (January 1997).
23 *National Consumer Council Report* (February 1997).
24 Robert Skidelsky, *The World After Communism* (Macmillan, 1995).

3 The State to Come

1 See John Gray, *False Dawn: The Utopia of the Global Free Market* (Granta Books, forthcoming); David Held, David Goldblatt, Anthony Mcgrew and Jonathan Perraton, *Global Flows, Global Transformation* (Open University, forthcoming); *The Politics of Globalisation* (Nexus Group, forthcoming).
2 Gray, *False Dawn*. Op. cit.
3 See W. Ruirok and R. van Tulder, *The Logic of International Restructuring* (Routledge, 1995); Paul Hirst and Grahame Thompson, *Globalisation in Question* (Polity, 1996).
4 George Bulkley and Richard Harris report in the *Economic Journal* (March 1997) that analysts are poor at forecasting company profits, and investors would do better to apply average estimates of profits to individual companies than to rely on analysts' forecasts.
5 See IPPR, *Promoting Prosperity: A Business Agenda for Britain* (Vintage, 1997).
6 Charles Leadbetter's inspiring book, *The Rise of the Social Entrepreneur* (Demos, 1997), gives some idea of the potential.
7 See *The British Spring* (Demos, April 1997)
8 See Alan Hughes et al, and their work at the ESRC Centre for Business Research, Cambridge.
9 Martin Weale of the National Institute of Economic and

Social Research estimates that taxation needs to rise by 2 per cent of GDP or £14 billion (*Observer*, 16 March 1997).

10 A forthcoming article in *Renewal* by David Halpern and Stuart White.

11 John Hills, *Private Welfare Insurance and Social Security: Pushing the Boundaries* (York Publishing Services, 1997).

4 And So to Europe

1 John Laughland makes this point in *The Tainted Source: The Undemocratic Origins of the European Idea* (Little, Brown, 1997)

2 See Kenneth Clarke's Chatham House speech in December 1996.

3 Professor David Currie gives a good overview as a 'pro sceptic' in *The Pros and Cons of EMU* (Economic Intelligence Unit, February 1997).

4 See *The British Spring* (Demos, April 1997).

INDEX

Also available in Vintage

The Commission on Social Justice

SOCIAL JUSTICE

STRATEGIES FOR NATIONAL RENEWAL

'Essential reading for everyone who wants a new way forward for our country'
Tony Blair

The UK needs new direction. We need to be clear about our values, understand the forces shaping change, create our own vision of the future – and then set out to achieve it. Our fate is not determined; we can bridge the gap between the country we are and the country we would like to be. This book shows how.

'John Smith's anger at the state of Britain today led him to establish the Commission on Social Justice. Its report will inform Labour's policy making and provide the basis for a vital national debate about the future of work and welfare. It is essential reading for everyone who wants a new way forward for our country'
Tony Blair MP

The Observer for half price, just 50p!

cash value 0.0001p

Complete this voucher, take it to your newsagent and pick up a copy of the Observer for only 50p.

Mr/Mrs/Miss/Ms ________ Initials ________________ Surname ____________________

Address ____

____ Postcode ________________

How many times a month do you buy the Observer? ☐

How many times a week do you buy the Guardian? ☐

If you don't wish to receive further information screened by the Guardian Media Group please tick ☐

Offer valid until 30 June 1997

The Observer for half price, just 50p!

cash value 0.0001p

Complete this voucher, take it to your newsagent and pick up a copy of the Observer for only 50p.

Mr/Mrs/Miss/Ms ________ Initials ________________ Surname ____________________

Address ____

____ Postcode ________________

How many times a month do you buy the Observer? ☐

How many times a week do you buy the Guardian? ☐

If you don't wish to receive further information screened by the Guardian Media Group please tick ☐

Offer valid until 30 June 1997

The Observer for half price, just 50p!

cash value 0.0001p

Complete this voucher, take it to your newsagent and pick up a copy of the Observer for only 50p.

Mr/Mrs/Miss/Ms ________ Initials ________________ Surname ____________________

Address ____

____ Postcode ________________

How many times a month do you buy the Observer? ☐

How many times a week do you buy the Guardian? ☐

If you don't wish to receive further information screened by the Guardian Media Group please tick ☐

Offer valid until 30 June 1997

The Observer for half price, just 50p!

cash value 0.0001p

Complete this voucher, take it to your newsagent and pick up a copy of the Observer for only 50p.

Mr/Mrs/Miss/Ms ________ Initials ________________ Surname ____________________

Address ____

____ Postcode ________________

How many times a month do you buy the Observer? ☐

How many times a week do you buy the Guardian? ☐

If you don't wish to receive further information screened by the Guardian Media Group please tick ☐

Offer valid until 30 June 1997

The Newsagent

Thank you for accepting this voucher which represents a discount of 50p from the normal price of the Observer. Please complete the details below and when you return this voucher to the wholesaler, your account will be credited with 50p plus 2p handling allowance. We are very grateful for your continuing co-operation.

Supplying Wholesaler ______________________

URN/Box Number ______________________

The Wholesaler

Please credit the returning newsagent with 52p (50p plus 2p handling allowance). Your account will be credited with 52p plus your normal handling allowance. Return completed vouchers to Mencap London Division.

The Newsagent

Thank you for accepting this voucher which represents a discount of 50p from the normal price of the Observer. Please complete the details below and when you return this voucher to the wholesaler, your account will be credited with 50p plus 2p handling allowance. We are very grateful for your continuing co-operation.

Supplying Wholesaler ______________________

URN/Box Number ______________________

The Wholesaler

Please credit the returning newsagent with 52p (50p plus 2p handling allowance). Your account will be credited with 52p plus your normal handling allowance. Return completed vouchers to Mencap London Division.

The Newsagent

Thank you for accepting this voucher which represents a discount of 50p from the normal price of the Observer. Please complete the details below and when you return this voucher to the wholesaler, your account will be credited with 50p plus 2p handling allowance. We are very grateful for your continuing co-operation.

Supplying Wholesaler ______________________

URN/Box Number ______________________

The Wholesaler

Please credit the returning newsagent with 52p (50p plus 2p handling allowance). Your account will be credited with 52p plus your normal handling allowance. Return completed vouchers to Mencap London Division.

The Newsagent

Thank you for accepting this voucher which represents a discount of 50p from the normal price of the Observer. Please complete the details below and when you return this voucher to the wholesaler, your account will be credited with 50p plus 2p handling allowance. We are very grateful for your continuing co-operation.

Supplying Wholesaler ______________________

URN/Box Number ______________________

The Wholesaler

Please credit the returning newsagent with 52p (50p plus 2p handling allowance). Your account will be credited with 52p plus your normal handling allowance. Return completed vouchers to Mencap London Division.